MW00815305

AFTER
THE
STATIC

By

Mark A. Mihalko

Cover Design and Layout by Brenda Mihalko

First Ringmaster's Realm Edition, September 2017

Published in the United States of America

ISBN-10:1545149208
ISBN-13:9781545149201

Forget ye not what was and is to be!
Flesh without sin, world without end!

– Anton LaVey

FORWARD

The End Times are an extremely polarizing topic. For some in society, they are nothing more than fictional events prophesized long ago that will never come true. Almost like a biblical representation of an apocalyptic boogeyman. For others, the End Times are very real, with strange markers popping up across the globe pointing to their beginning. Are they real? That is a question for the ages.

Looking around society here in the United States, that answer could be yes, as our once great nation is fractured and bleeding at the seams. Although it has been building for some time, the differing ideologies and opinions alive in our country have created a great rift among the population. This divide, coupled with the volumes of misinformation being broadcast daily by the media, and confusion reigns supreme.

Not since the Civil War have we experienced so much brother-against-brother strife. Families are being torn apart as parts of society fights for their side of the agenda. Gone are the days of discussion, where thought-out conversations could be had to make sense of the happenings. Instead, acts of civil disobedience, protests, and violence have consumed the narrative. Because of this, as a nation we may be spiraling to the brink of the End Days, all we need is a spark.

Unfortunately, no matter which side of the debate you favor, discovering the truth is becoming harder every day. Fake news is everywhere, and it is up to all of us as individuals to decipher what is true and what is false; this is a battle in and to itself. The media cannot be trusted, journalism is dead, and blogs all point to a single side of a topic steered by the writers' worldview. Sure, this is nothing new, but as the days pass by, the environment is growing more antagonistic and hostile.

When I sat down and started this project, these problems were not so bad or as noticeable as they are today. Only a couple of years ago the shadows of the truth were hidden in the open for the entire world to see if they looked. Today, that curtain has fallen and another curtain exists. Fortunately, while this game of hiding the truth has become somewhat more difficult, sure signs have become recognizable. The rise of (and reliance on) technology has allowed many in society to bypass this shroud and expose the dark realities that exist. False flag operations that would once torment societies for generations are now easily debunked, thus allowing people to wake to the global technocracy that is overtaking the world.

At heart, this is the New World Order President Bush referred to during speeches in the 1990s. A one-world government is not out for the good of humanity, but for the destruction of societies and complete global domination by any means necessary. If you look at it, everything makes sense and the end game of the twisted experimentation of the 1900s apparent. Now, a new enemy lay ahead and the worlds' leaders back them.

The miserable part is that there are still millions of people walking our planet in denial. Greed, power, control, everything is at the disposal of these monsters, and no one on Earth is now safe from the reach of their tentacles, but still, it is just a conspiracy theory. Sadly, for those blind individuals, gone are the days of the cover black ops centered in modernized nations.

Now, an era of uncontrolled experimentations has been ushered in under the blue and white flag of the eugenicists, and the global elite infects millions in the underdeveloped third world nations. Haven't you noticed the rise of vile pandemics across the globe? I have, and for what, population control? Their agenda etched in stone for all humanity to see; a world of 500 million is what the Guidestones call for, and they believe that number is still attainable even with a worldwide population of 7.4 billion.

As I sit here near completion of this project, I am witnessing an awakening of sorts. People across the globe are rising to the challenge and are finally speaking out against this repressive monstrosity. Sure, it isn't easy; it's met with cries of outrage and a fear of repercussions for speaking out against the mind controlled masses, but it must be done if we all want to survive. In the United Kingdom, you had BREXIT, and in the United States, Donald Trump defeated Hillary Clinton mostly due to his campaign to place America first instead of bowing to the globalist programs supported by the last four puppets to hold office. Both of these movements followed the voice of the people (even if the Left is crying about the popular vote), and are giving society a chance to defeat the elites that are continually positioning nations against each other so to reap the rewards when their manmade chaos erupts.

While this work is based on a fictional set of events taking place inside a small, somewhat isolated, portion of the United States, the actual premise may not be far fetched as we cannot dismiss or ignore the overall power of the globalist machine. It is not impossible that similar activities aren't taking place right now in one of the many financially and technology deprived nations in the underdeveloped world. These people are evil, and they will not rest until humanity falls to their knees.

I for one did not spend 21-years protecting our nation to watch some non-American bureaucrat come in and try to destroy our country or make a mockery out of our sovereign rights granted under the Constitution. To them, remember this, I am not alone in my desire to stand against your attempts to infringe upon our inalienable rights and the resistance you will face while attempting this maneuver will be stronger than you could have ever perceived. I will stand against the global elites to protect our sovereignty and lead the fight to help wake the rest of the sleeping giants brainwashed by decades of propaganda. I will not enter this battle alone; I know many more individuals that feel the same way.

To that end, this manuscript is quite real, and inside these pages, I have revealed some hard truths that may seem shocking. Even the blog mentioned inside is real and holds more information for you to dig into (survivingstatic.blogspot.com). Sure, some people may disregard some of the material and call it nothing but a "Conspiracy Theory," but from years of research, these theories have been proven to be fact. They are disgusting truths hidden within the shroud of the global agenda and the reality that the world must wake to. Just remember, all hope is not lost, and our awakening is just beginning,

- Mark A. Mihalko

DEDICATION

This work is dedicated to the dead and undead voices that have both influenced and motivated me throughout my journey toward enlightenment. Without all of you and my Brothers and Sisters in the Goat Locker, the truths of this unseen war would have remained silent. Navy Chief, Navy Pride!

CHAPTERS

PROLOGUE

"The First Angel Went and Poured Out His Bowl on the Earth"

Creatures of the night surround us
Romero laughs
His diabolic vision of despair
Of humor and laughter
A misleading masterpiece for those
willing to understand the genius

Strangers unite
Fighting a plague of humanity before they fall prey
Victims, not innocent, but oblivious of their sins
Their cannibalistic nature striking fear in us all
Not because of the sheer terror
Or their horrific deeds
But, for the primal nature lurking at our core

The taste of flesh as sweet as the fruit on the vine
The lure, the only difference
Or is it?
Instead of a snake in the garden
We are persuaded by desire
Carnal temptations leading us to flesh

At the heart, the snake and the pleasures are equal
These forbidden dreams considered taboo
So misunderstood, that the thought alone
often spawns remorse
A lingering guilt that creates hatred
And yes, these monsters for us to cheer

The screens are full of surrealistic views of reality
Where the creatures indulge in the carnal feasts,
we covet
Where one's flesh and blood replaces the
love and hate, we hold on a pedestal
In many ways, we are all alike
Zombies searching for companionship
instead of brains
Embracing the taste of our lover's
skin during passion

For us, our time is here;
the day of reckoning is now
The Apocalypse has begun

**CHAPTER
ONE**

"TO SHEW UNTO HIS SERVANTS THINGS
WHICH MUST SHORTLY COME TO PASS…"

OCTOBER 2

The poetic introduction to this manuscript may seem a bit strange, but when you dive into your mind, you will realize everything you know about strange flesh eating outbreaks and a zombie apocalypse can be traced to the fictional world. There is nothing wrong with this in any way, especially when one considers the massive increase in entertainment and video games making the subject commonplace over the past few decades. Did you ever wonder why? I will admit I never did, but maybe I should have.

Everywhere you look, you can see an example of the modern zombie, as portrayed in books, films, and, games. Not surprisingly, the mutated creatures are quite different from the descriptions depicted in their source materials found in actual documented cases of the undead Voodoo zombies and those found in other international folklore. The contemporary zombies typically portrayed in popular culture as mindless, unfeeling monsters with a hunger for human flesh is completely off base; as is the idea that these creatures can sustain damage far beyond that of an average living human and can pass their infection onto others. This prototype was established in the seminal 1968 film *Night of the Living Dead* and has remained virtually unchanged ever since.

After this emotional movie, zombies would only be seen overwhelming society in mobs and waves, living only to eat by seeking blood, flesh, intestines, or any other human limb possible. Typically, they would show signs of physical decomposition with rotting flesh, discolored eyes, and open wounds, and move in somewhat stylized, yet unusual ways. They are incapable of communication, showing no signs of personality, rationality or any ability of reason, They also seemed to lack the abilities to organize, run, or swim. In many cases, these fiends are closely tied to the idea of a zombie apocalypse. For some, this is already taking place in our world with the collapse of civilization from a vast plague of undead being silenced by a complicit media.

There are a few other examples from the entertainment industry, while they are closer to the truth; yet, they do not have the same influence in shaping beliefs. Even today, one can still find differences among the depictions of zombies by various media; for one comparison see the contrasts between zombies by Night of the Living Dead authors George A. Romero and John A. Russo as they evolved in the two separate film series that followed. The unfortunate truth is that the seeds planted by the entertainment industry are now firmly linked to the zombie mythos that there are very few instances of the beasts that show them in any other context.

So, before I get rolling into the heart of this book, I wanted to run through a quick overview of the real zombie mythos to show that there was something much more sinister involved in what we experienced during the pandemic. When a person wants to dive into the heart of a zombie, they must take a thorough look at the Voodoo religion. According to the tenets of Voodoo, a Bokor or Voodoo sorcerer can revive the dead. These Zombies remain under the control of the bokor since they have no will of their own. An excellent example of this from pop culture is the classic film *White Zombie.*

One timeless case can be found in 1937, where Zora Neale Hurston while researching folklore in Haiti, encountered the case of Felicia Felix-Mentor, who had died was buried, and returned in 1907 at the age of 29. Hurston pursued rumors that the affected persons were given powerful drugs, but she was unable to locate individuals willing to offer much information.

Several decades later, Wade Davis, a Canadian ethnobotanist, presented a pharmacological case for zombies in two books, *The Serpent and the Rainbow* (1985) and *Passage of Darkness: The Ethnobiology of the Haitian Zombie* (1988). Davis traveled to Haiti in 1982 and as a result of his inquiries came to the conclusion that a living person can be transformed into a zombie when two special powders are entered into the blood stream. After this trip, he also popularized the story of Clairvius Narcisse, who claimed to have succumbed to this practice.

Others have discussed the contribution of the victim's belief system, possibly leading to compliance with the attacker's will, causing psychogenic amnesia, catatonia, or other psychological disorders, which are later misinterpreted as a return from the dead. Scottish psychiatrist R. D. Laing further highlighted the link between social and cultural expectations and compulsion, in the context of schizophrenia and other mental illness, suggesting that schizogenesis may account for some of the psychological aspects of zombification.

While these were some investigations and theories, the idea of the zombie dates back even further. In the Middle Ages, it was commonly believed that the souls of the dead could return to earth and haunt the living. The belief in revenants (someone who has returned from the dead) is well documented by contemporary European writers of the time, such as William of Newburgh and Walter Map. This creature, the revenant, would usually take the form of an emaciated corpse wandering through the ancient graveyards at night. Accounts can also be traced to medieval Norse mythology, as well as several other cultures worldwide, including China, Japan, the Pacific, India, and the Native Americans. However, the most famous and popularized cases sit in Haiti within the mysterious Voodoo religion.

The word Voodoo derives from the word Vodu in the Fon language of Dahomey meaning spirit or god and describes the complex religious and belief system that exist in Haiti, an island of the West Indies. The foundations of Voodoo were established in the seventeenth century by slaves captured primarily from the Kingdom of Dahomey, which occupied parts of today's Togo, Benin, and Nigeria in West Africa. This religion combines features of Native African religious practices with the Roman Catholicism that was practiced by the European settlers.

Unfortunately, in literature and film, Voodoo has been reduced to sorcery, black magic, and in some cases even cannibalistic practices, poisoning many against the practice. In reality, this religious practice includes the belief in a supreme God (Bon Dieu) and a host of spirits called Loa, which are often identified analog to many of the saints revered by the Catholic Church. Many of these spirits are closely related to African Gods, and many represent natural phenomena such as fire, water, or the wind and can even signify eminent ancestors.

One belief that is fully embraced by the followers of voodoo is the zombie. The Creole word Zombi is apparently derived from Nzambi, a West African deity. Incredibly, this view can only be traced back to 1929, after the publication of William B. Seabrook's *The Magic Island*. In this book, Seabrook recounts his experiences on Haiti, including witnessing the walking dead.

Unlike the modern zombies popularized today, Haitian zombies were once ordinary people, but underwent zombification by a Bokor, through a spell or potion. The victim then dies and returns, becoming a monotonous mechanism, incapable of remembering the past, unable to identify loved ones, and condemned to a life serving the will of the zombie master.

This practice can be seen throughout history in Haiti, with no one more notorious than Papa Doc Duvalier, the dictator of Haiti from 1957 to 1971, who had a private army referred to as Tonton Macoutes. These entranced soldiers followed his every command and seemed to be under his spell. It was also a well-known fact that Duvalier also had his own Voodoo Church and he promised his parishioners that he would return after his death to rule again. While that never happened, a guard was placed at the entrance of his tomb to ensure he could not escape or no one was able to gain access and steal his body.

As you can tell from this small synopsis of zombie lore, we could sit here and dissect the validity of this topic for months or even years. As you will come to find, some of the situations encountered by some of us that survived during this silenced outbreak may not entirely fall into the classic zombie mythos as outlined, but some strange similarities haunt us all these years later. No matter what the cause, something very strange took place during that time and the way the events ran parallel to many different religious beliefs seem to be the real mystery. Could Voodoo have been involved or was there something darker and more sinister at work? These are great questions that can only be answered at the end of our journey. Please, sit back and join me on this trip back into this nightmare.

**CHAPTER
TWO**

"AND THE FIFTH ANGEL
BLEW HIS TRUMPET..."

OCTOBER 4

In many ways, the story I am about to relay mirrors the obscene realities popularized today and yesteryear in pop culture. However, unlike those fictional tales of undead atrocities, the following descriptions and accounts are real, taken from eyewitness testimony, audio recordings, and personal experience of the events beginning on February 13, 2014. That sad day will live forever inside those of us that somehow survived, in those of us that dealt with the vile darkness that overtook our beloved city.

While some of the documents I am working from are scraps of papers found throughout the ordeal, others are intact and include visuals that I can't put into words. For those and some of the videos, I have created a blog that you could visit to see some of the supporting documents. That blog can be found at survivingthestatic.blogspot.com; you should check it out if you have a chance; you may find something interesting or take solace in some of the standalone accounts that didn't make it into this volume of stories.

How did it start, what agency created this plague, was it the United Nations, or was it something biblical? These are but some of the questions that will forever haunt my thoughts. Even now, as I document the information at hand, information that could one day solve the greater mystery that is entwined in the depths of this horrific account.

Every day for the last three months, I have awoken to the visions of blood soaked snow that soiled the cobblestone streets; the never-ending nightmare that I can't forget. Those prophetic visions are pushing me to complete this manuscript, to tell these stories. Where should I begin? Let me see, maybe here with this strange account. From my research, this video recording could be the scientists' responsible for the outbreak talking about patient zero.

I

(Play) *I can't believe that the impossible has happened. One of the specimens managed to endure the process, surviving to see the light of day. It mutated beyond our capacity to conceive. Our agenda never allowed for their freedom after vaccination, the world is far from ready to comprehend the truth, to discover our manic exploitation of the meek. The gates of ridicule would open, and we would all be ruined.*

Why were we so stupid, after the devastation of the battles, all the death, and smoldering bodies? I still cannot believe it. How could we leave Sector Two unguarded? Idiots, they are all idiots. The best security money can buy, honestly? I know that it's what those feeble old men said in their brief. I listened, although I knew we should have taken more precautions. We're smarter than that. Now, the disease is free. Our only hope is the quarantine or eradication of the contagion, whatever comes first.

I will not believe what we see from the plane overhead. Oh God, it is as if the gates of Hell have opened my eyes. The virus is spreading throughout the city. At this rate, quarantine is impossible. These vile creatures are everywhere. The outbreak is uncontrollable. This can't be happening, what have we done? What have I created? Our plans are evaporating right in front of our eyes; we must escape this vessel before the others awaken before we become their experiment in pleasure, their host. Our facility is not safe, sound the evacuation alarm! We're ruined; there is no escape! We are doomed! **(Stop).**

II

Damn it, NO MORE... I can't take this anymore. Why am I doing this, what am I thinking? (Silence)...

Oh, sorry about that. Let me tell you, although I survived these atrocities, in many ways, I am a shell of myself, and this project is opening some very sore wounds. After watching this video, it is clear that the scientists were more concerned with their reputation or financial wealth than the outcome of terror that was at hand. A terror that as everyone soon discovered was far more advanced than they could recognize. As disturbing as the recounting of the video above, the following encounter found in a building outside of the city may be even more riveting. This account (from a digital recorder at the thrift store) demonstrates that these creatures not only could think for themselves, it appears that they also possessed feelings that could be perceived as human.

(Click) 11 o'clock, another body falls. This strange infection continues to grow, surrounding our every move. Look, in the corner by the rusty pipe, such a ghastly sight. Those red eyes filled with sorrow, that festering decay of the green death. His body ravaged by the toxin. How can he exist? Who would want to live that way? Stealthily, I maintain my distance. I will not fall prey to this vile demon; the rot will not overtake me.

Turning the corner, I see even more victims carousing throughout the corridor, their infestation searching for hosts like zombies for brains. Only a few of us remain active on this funeral barge along the river, defying the poisonous torture. How much longer can we survive in this floating prison? Our friends destroyed, yet our search for the cure must continue. 11:30, another man falls. No one is safe, our lives ruined, all hope lost!

Tonight I must escape; the atrocities that surround me are closing in. This terror, this infection, what have they done to us? This hunger is erupting from deep inside my bowels, why do I crave it so? My lips moisten at the mere thought. If I didn't know better, I would think, I know I will not survive another night on here. I can feel them near; our pulse seems to beat in unison, why? Where has my mind gone? My eyes grow weary. My skin, something seems wrong with my skin. That taste. I cannot shake this craving, what is happening to me? What have they done to us? Look, over there in the light, that doorway, my escape, freedom at last.

Wait, what is that crawling in the corner? Could it be another like me? Could they too be searching for salvation? There it is again... That hunger. It's calling me.

What have they done to me? My pulse quickens. I can hear the echoes of my heart stir, pulsating through my now placid flesh. Me, it cannot be, no, I will never quarry. The door, I must reach the door. Once I get some air, I'll be okay. I'll wake from this torment, this nightmare. Two more steps, which is all I need until deliverance. The air, it'll cleanse me of these thoughts. Free me from the desires that are overwhelming my senses. There it is again, that hunger. What is it? My hands, oh god! They, no, the rot! Damn them to hell. What did they do to me?

I don't know what has come over me. All I know is that in five seconds, I will be free of this barge, this chamber of despair. I must compose myself. Once I leave, there is no turning back. Not for me, not for them. I may be the only one left coherent enough to escape exile, to see the blood red skies of our future. Funny, I can't feel the door, I am pushing, and I know I am.

There it is again, that hunger, drawing me closer to those bystanders next to the phone booth. Maybe one of them could call a taxi for me. The light is brighter than I expected. That hunger, how the pains grow inside of me. Why couldn't I feel the door? My hands, they are, wait, look what they have done to my hands. I must move on. They can't catch me now. Somehow, I must find a way to blend in with those people.

As I close in, I worry; will they notice my hands? Will they pity me for the infestation created by the re-animators? They can't! I will not let them. There it is again, that bitter taste plaguing my every move, the anguish grows with every step. I can smell it now, fragrantly alive all around me. Oh no, it cannot be that.

The blonde-haired woman in the front, I know, it is from her. What is it? What is so tempting? I can't take it much longer, my stomach, my eyes, and these thoughts. I have to control myself. I need to figure out what these monsters have done. There she is. At last, our hearts beat in tandem. Yesterday, I would've gladly walked up to her. Now, now, I feel a swarm running through my veins, my blood flows with an unnatural bitterness

Am I alive, I do not feel like it, I feel dead inside like I'm rotting from my entrails! My hands, I cannot believe my hands. I reach for her. "Help me," her scream pierces the thin serene air. My heart races, my glands salivate. She smells so delicious. I cannot control myself any longer; I must have her. Oh god, oh, Lord, what have I done? What am I doing? I cannot stop this frenzy. She... she tastes so sweet. Her brains... Her blood, her soul **(click).**

III

It is amazing how these two accounts seem to originate from the same location, but where? There was that World Health Organization (WHO) facility along the north side of the Allegheny. That would make sense, as countries such as India and Ethiopia have felt the wrath of their vaccination program on children. Hell, even the Ebola outbreak in Liberia can be traced to back to them, or at least their parent organization the United Nations (with help from the CDC and that globalist Bill Gales); although, the Ebola pandemic did have more to do with diamonds than depopulation. And Zika, their biggest success, was only successful because of the brain-dead populace that could not see the actual meaning hidden in the chemtrails.

What is more disturbing though is this next slice of evidence I dug up (and yes I mean dug up from a reporter that was not as lucky). It appears that their vile bodies had an intellect that rose far above what we could believe possible. Plus, it seems that they had friends in high places (United Nations?). That's right, according to this video; they could organize. It appears that these demonic forces were together not only for an assault on unsuspecting society but of religion as well. It is hard to imagine creatures speaking the words of scripture that never existed; yet, their leader in his bright blue and white vestments was using his pulpit to spread his gospel.

I do have to warn you, though, most of the scripture in these accounts had to be translated from Latin. While I do have some understanding of the language from reading old textbooks and translation guides, I'm by no means an expert. Unfortunately, my subpar high school did not offer it (even as an elective). For those of you that may have a better understanding of that classic language, I have posted the Latin versions next to these verses on the blog that I mentioned earlier in this chapter. Plus, I will add all of the Latin passages from the Gospel in an addendum at the end of the manuscript.

There will be a day when the Earth will
tremble, and my prophecy will live,
Fear will overtake the damned and a lone
scream will be heard as our minion rise

(The Revelation of Moloch 1.11)

Everywhere I look, I see perfection. Around every corner, our congregation grows by harvesting the sinners for our blessed grey Communion. Or is it red, or green, does it really matter? Their succulent Eucharist tastes so sweet on my tongue. At least, appeasing my hunger for a few seconds before, the urge explodes inside me. My appetite is unfathomable, I want more of this flesh; more of this tender host.

The others, the nonconformists, the degenerates; they harbor this delicacy shrouding it beneath their porous temples. With most of them discarding their importance by destroying the texture. Yet, their mark... that symbol, what gives them the right? Even the ability to follow such an inane spirit seals their fate. To think, they believe they are safe, protected from the purification of their sins. True, they have been chosen.

Chosen, not by their excuse as a savior, but, by my followers.

Come, my disciples gather around. Do you hear that sound of panic vibrating throughout our cathedral? One of our brothers managed to free himself. Opening the door for the world to hear our sermon, to conform to our commandments. The frail, the beautiful, guilty I say, all guilty. However, their transgressions can be forgiven and their confessions heard upon the mount. I will give them absolution, and possibly, immortality.
Let us pray.

Lord of Light
I stand before you searching for the
guidance to lead my drove
Our hearts are open to the light you

Mark A. Mihalko

shine brightly upon the heavens
Our minds are open to the love you share
with your faithful concubine
Guide us through these dark, violent days
Giving us the composure to spread
your name throughout the world
Our time has finally arrived
In your name, we pray
Amen

**CHAPTER
THREE**

**"THEN A GREAT AND MYSTERIOUS
SIGHT APPEARED IN THE SKY …"**

OCTOBER 6

Sorry about the abrupt ending yesterday, the longer
I wrote the more disturbing the images became.
My mind is weak, and I started to relive that day,
that horror. I had to lay down; the terrifying visions
began to become real. I never want to be part of that
nightmare again; I want to move on.

So where was I, oh, yeah, there? It seems as though
the accounts were not entirely centered on those who
were infected or were responsible. After some digging,
I was able to come into a diary of an innocent and her
child. Still, there are times when the following is too
much. However, her story must be told.

I

February 13, 2014

*Baby, I decided to stop and take a break and
write down some of what is happening just incase
something happens to me out here, Trust me, I wish*

none of this happened, but you need to know the truth. I will do everything in my power to make sure you are safe. You mean more to me than anything and I will stop at nothing to make sure your birth goes as smoothly as possible.

What are those evil creatures? Where did they come from? Their skin, their faces... My god, their faces! Give me strength Lord to escape. To escape their atrocities, I alone am insignificant, a soulless vessel drifting aimlessly upon these blood stained corridors'. But, you my son, Eli, you will be different. I just know you will be. I can feel your greatness pulsate throughout my womb; I am aware that your destiny lies on a different path than mine.

Once I start to move again, where do I turn? The streets are overrun by that demonic hoard. I must escape the city. Maybe they are isolated here, trapped by the rotting stench of decay. The water, yes, the water, it will protect me. I saw it once in a movie. That's right, I remember it so clearly. These zombies cannot cross the water. I must head to the west once I get to the crossroad next to the gas station.

Hold on baby; Momma will protect you. Momma will make things right for you. Damn your father. Isaac, why did you run off with that petty whore? What could she give him that I, we, could not? It's his loss, though. Just remember that after you are born, when you become a man, a leader. Until then, rely on my guidance; you are my world.

There it is, the Bridge. If I remember correctly, there is a small cottage about six miles ahead. Not far from that worn-down cemetery where we would picnic. That was the first time your father, well, you do not need to hear about that. Where are all of the cars? Strange, it should be rush hour if my watch is right. Yes, rush hour, yet, this highway is empty. We cannot be the only ones left. Others had to have made it through the city after the explosion. Hmmm, I know we will.

II

Her emotion was so real; I could feel her fear. I could taste the tension in her voice and her thoughts. Why would the world be so cruel? If there is a God, he definitely was not on her side that day. If anything, he left her and the unborn child as a human sacrifice. This was strange behavior for a supposed divine being, although, he did leave his son rot on a cross inside a crown of thorns. Maybe, he is not so divine after all.

While her tale was just beginning, the victim from the first account seems to have escaped the facility he was in and is still struggling with what is happening. Evidently, he is still unaware of the depth of the transformation that is taking place within him. He sees himself alive; he can still talk, or at least think aloud.

(Click) What is wrong with me? These thoughts, these feelings, I am alive, yet I do not feel. What happened to me last night? My mind is a swirling reservoir of desire, craving not you alone, but your flesh like never before. Gabrielle, darling, why do you flee with our child in your womb? I can feel your heartbeat; hear the sweet elixir pulsate through your veins, calling out to me. It is whispering hints of the perfection, you harbor. Come back take me. Take all of me; I am yours. But, these thoughts, they haunt me, draining the essence of my instincts to an almost animalistic state, driving me to the edge of reason.

Why do I not long for your touch or the flavor of your inner thighs? Strangely, I cannot remember anything like that or who you are for that matter. I just know you exist, wandering out there waiting to complete me. I am drawn by the scent of your mental decay; the forbidden nectar that I long to taste, the tissue I long to devour. My lips moisten at the hint of your flesh. Will you let me ravage you, let us finally become one? I must break through the fog that surrounds me. I must find you.

*The others that escaped the facility will help me, we think as one. We share similar desires to feed on the despair, to have our way with you. Pleasuring you as only we can, taking you to the edge of satisfaction where the pain turns to ecstasy. We are coming for you, hoping you will willingly join us in our endeavor. You have nothing to fear, we all love you. Please, do not hide from us; our reunion is inevitable. Your brains will taste so sweet! **(Click).***

Sorry, I cannot type anymore. However, I know I must continue this manuscript. This story must be told, the victims, the perpetrators must become known. Not tonight, though, these visions are so clear, so terrifying. Gabrielle, who is this Gabrielle, and why is she so important?

**CHAPTER
FOUR**

"THE SECOND HORROR IS OVER, BUT
THE THIRD HORROR WILL COME SOON…"

OCTOBER 10

Finally, I am back at my computer. I never thought
that I would make it today, between traffic, therapy,
and a stop at the survivor's hospice, it seemed like
my day would never end. Although, I did discover
some interesting facts that will eventually find their
way into this novel. It is strange, for some reason I
see my compilation of details being dismissed by the
masses as a work of fiction. I honestly cannot believe
how they are treating the survivors at that facility.
They appear to be suffering more today from the
medications then they were from the delusions and
the memories that drove them to the hospital in the
first place. At least, a few of us continue to visit and
give them the real support they deserve. Fucking
socialistic government, rot in Hell.

After all, I believe in time we will discover that the
anti-American regime that is running this country
is at fault for the destruction. I know it was their
experiments that went awry (with their partners at

the United Nations), not some private corporation like is circling the underground rumor mill. How else could no official documents survive? The government must be covering up the truth. That is not surprising; they did it with Roswell, JFK, and even Flight 800 (we will skip 9-11, but that too falls into their twisted world view). The power of the military industrial complex is so far reaching; they must be exposed. With that in mind, let us get back to our scientists, those fucking geeks that created this disorder...

I

(Play) Damn it, men, get your asses in gear. Can't you hear those monsters closing in on us? You have seen their ferocity; the way they can sense us a mile away. If we do not get out of here soon, we will be dinner. Strange, I never considered myself a main course; what would I be? Well, there was that time in Vegas. Damn it, what am I doing? They will be here soon.

John, Paul, Mark come with me. When I designed this facility, I planned an escape route just in case some high-level brass wanted to shut us down. Those pansy bureaucrats always panic if they have the inkling of something going awry. Mark, grab as many of those records as possible, we will definitely need that to have any semblance of a clue to what is happening. Hey, pass me that laptop. Damn, those groans, that smell, its...

Directions, yes, just incase we are separated during our getaway; here are the routes. We will be safer in numbers (at least I think so). Head down the main hallway to the wall with the triple arrows. At the arrows, push on the exit sign in the ceiling. There, you will see a passageway. Follow it to the Boulevard of the Allies. Just be sure that none of those maggots are following you. From there, head west to the Fort Pitt Tunnel, we will meet there.

Although this situation is regrettably tragic, this is our, what in hell am I saying? I deserve this; this is my creation. The work must continue; we cannot go out like this. We are ever so close to perfecting this serum. It is still hard to believe how the toxin took hold once crystallization started. I cannot wait to find some solitude and dive into the data; I must scour the data and try to find the error

Come on people hurry your ass -I hear-those moans. That putrid smell, decay; they are catching up to us. Damn, I wish I had my gun. I would love to carry a specimen with us. However, we are too far from the lab, and it is not worth the risk. Maybe if we are lucky, we can snag one by the cottage. I think the cottage will be safe; I have not seen anyone on that road since. Since-well- Never mind... **(Stop)**

II

As those spineless weasels ran for their lives in fear of their creation, it seems as if there was an army forming from the ever-increasing number of infected. As I mentioned earlier, their leader, that tall, pale-skinned man, appeared to have an intellect instilled from above. However, it is strange, the more research I do, the more evidence I find proving that this is no accident. It could be possible that something more secular could be involved.

Upon the day the pure rise and
across the mighty river
Our saviors will meet in a grotto
at the base of the mount
The boon will shed a lone tear in the garden
And the screams of the sinners will echo
throughout the new city

(The Revelation of Moloch 2.10)

Look, my children and listen. I can see the brilliance of our labor at hand, as the prophecy of our lord, my father, is before us. Behold the new day go forth and spread our gospel to the infidels. Enlighten their feeble minds with pain and pleasure. Soon, our congregation will take root in every corner of the globe, and there all of our thoughts and prayers will unify.

Our brother Luke started preaching the word last night. He went out into the depths of the unholy, converting the unwilling to our path. Join him by increasing our army of prayer warriors and cleansing the offenders of their indiscretions and strengthening our determination.

Luke appeared to me last night. He helped me visualize his odyssey into Satan's depths. What impurities he encountered as the atrocities surrounded him. And, his resolve remained steadfast. Let us pray.

Lord of Light
Watch over your flock as we travel forth
into the abyss
Challenging the faithless to repent their misdeeds
Opening their hearts, to the fulfillment
only you can provide

Opening their minds, to the direction
only you can lead
Give us your strength and courage
to spread your will
Guiding us across the horizon to another
land of despair for us to conquer
With your desire burning through our veins
we shall never fail
In your name, we pray
Amen

III

See what I mean, his words seem to project a wisdom set down many years before this ordeal. Note to self; I need to do more research on the preacher. Who he was, where he came from? For some reason, his words resonate deep within the core of my soul. Every time, I sit down to type another entry involving him, I want to stand and fight as well...

Now, back to the original task, documenting the events that our government says never occurred. When I am done, they will never be able to deny the reality of the situation. Where do I go? I think it is time to get back to our innocent victim and her unborn. I still cannot imagine what it could be like dealing with all of this while carrying something so special.

February 14, 2014

I had to stop again; you are too heavy for me to be carrying on foot. I can't believe that there are so many assholes out here. Sorry about the language, but it is the truth. I know we all need to escape, but I cannot believe how they just sped by, that burnt smell from the tires is still etched into my mind.

A few minutes ago before I stopped, I thought I saw Esther's car. She was nowhere to be found though. That's a shame, if she were there, she would have helped us, even if she did. Plus, she may have known where your father is. I called for her, but all I heard was silence. There were no signs of Esther or your dad anywhere. Hopefully, we find them safe. Your father Isaac may be a bastard, but I still love him.

Actually, you should know that he would make a great dad if he would settle down. The booze, the drugs, and the women; if he does not realize the error of his ways soon, he will end up dead. Who knows, he may be dead already. If these savages didn't devour him in the street, his new addiction might have. It is definitely worse than ecstasy (not that you know what that is). And to think, his supplier is some government scientist that works black ops for the CIA (at least that's what your dad told me). Crazy, scientist, and drug dealer, what a great combination?

Alright baby, we are almost at the tunnel. I hope that none of those cannibals are inside when we get there; it would make for a short trip if there were. Maybe, we could scale Mount Washington or maybe the incline instead. Which one of those would be safer? No, we will have to take the tunnel; that is our only choice in my condition.

Damn, you are heavy! Remember that when you are all grown, your wife is with child, and you want to go hiking or something. You will understand. Wow, that was one hell of a kick! I have never felt a pain like that before. I am going to take a nap now, we have been on the go for the past 16 hours, and I am exhausted. You would too if you... Oh well, Happy Valentines Day baby. I love you.

...Wait, those sounds that smell. Oh, God! They are coming!

IV

Damn it, there are those thoughts again, those voices. Why do I torture myself with this stuff? Why should I be the one that has to experience this all over again? I cannot take it anymore; I do not want to go back there, I do not want to see those people again.

Goodnight all, hopefully, I can return tomorrow to continue my journey. Hopefully, I can regain focus. I have to!

**CHAPTER
FIVE**

**"AND AS SOON AS I HAD EATEN IT,
MY BELLY WAS BITTER..."**

OCTOBER 12

I know that I should be focusing on the manuscript today, but I can't these voices are killing me. They are making it impossible for me to do anything. Today has been one of the worst days I can remember, and it has been ALL day. They were so bad earlier that I lost my mind at group down at the clinic and had a total meltdown. I almost left altogether, with the visions of dismembered bodies lining the room feeling completely real. It was miserable, and I could taste the bile from my stomach rise with every breath.

If it weren't for my group partner Natalie, I would have fled. Not only did she talk me down and comfort me, somehow she was able to convince the voices to leave me alone even when all of the medication and water seemed to fail me. Natalie is a godsend. Over the past few months, she has gone out of her way to help me become purposeful again.

I know if it weren't for her, I wouldn't be here right now, and I would still be jumping at the sight of my own shadow.

In many ways, I wish I were stronger. At least, I am starting to feel alive again. I can honestly admit that I haven't been myself since the outbreak and I am definitely a shell of the man I once was. I once had confidence and carried myself like I was going to make a difference. Not anymore, Hell, I am afraid to ask her out to dinner. Maybe it's still the thought of Renae. I bet you she would approve, though, there is no way she would want me to suffer alone. Plus, in many ways, they are the same. Light blue eyes, pale skin, humble yet confident; they could be twins.

The only real difference is that Natalie is still alive. She was able to survive these merciless trials and tell the world her story. I am just thankful that these revolting beasts did not stain all of the beauty in this city and attractive women such as Natalie remain. Deep inside, I know that she would taste delicious, but her presence is enough nourishment for my soul.

What should I do? I want to ask her out to dinner, but I'm afraid rejection. What would she say? Would she say yes? There is no way; she has seen me at my worst; my insanity, my pain, and all of my struggles within this new reality. I'm sure she could never embrace who I am inside right now. At least I have our group sessions to pacify my desires. The clinic allows me a chance to steal a subtle glance or an accidental touch; if I am really lucky, maybe she will rub my shoulders to drive away the voices, and help me feel again.

What should I do? I have no clue. I had all intentions of writing some of the stories tonight, but I can't get my mind on track. For the first time in forever, the visions and voices have left me alone tonight and I probably should try to get some sleep and take advantage of the silence. I just wish I wasn't so alone.

Good night everyone, I promise I will return refreshed tomorrow prepared to dive deeper into the accounts that lay before us.

CHAPTER SIX

"I DID NOT SEE A TEMPLE IN THE CITY..."

October 20

Another night and another nightmare, I do not understand, when they come on, the terror chases me into the corner of my room. This house is so empty now with out you. Damn, I miss you. Sorry, I was just reminiscing about my days before the atrocities, before the military industrial complex (or fucking United Nations) started pushing their Agenda 21 sustainability bullshit. Like many, I lost quite a few friends and loved ones during the reaping, and my life was forever changed. At least, I have survived to lead a semi-normal life. From what the doctors tell me, I have a great chance at a full recovery.

Well, enough about me. Where was I when I left off? Him, well, that is not very bad. His account has at least been full of love, anguish, and an underlying bond. However, I still cannot understand how he does not realize what he is becoming. It is amazing, almost as if he is blocking it out; transporting himself to another time and place. Yes, that has to be the case; at least, that is the case with this next account; he almost hides the fact that he is a fucking flesh-eating bastard. Not only that, but he still seems to be searching for Gabrielle. Who is Gabrielle? I wonder, is she still alive? Shut up, stop the blood; please. Damn, must be time for my medication. Now, where did I put that yellow UPMC bottle; it must be here somewhere. Oh, there it is. Where, oh, yeah, back to the story.

I

(Click) Who are you, my vision of beauty? You still seem so familiar to me. Honestly, I feel as if I can sense your every move; experience your every fear. I can see you standing there by that torn CDC test notification on the building. Damn, if I never would have seen it in the first place. Maybe we would be in each other's arms. I can see you trembling at the horrid sights before you. Did one of my brothers do that? What am I saying, do I need to ask?

At last, the tunnel to the Promised Land, there our union, our destiny, and our reality all lay before us. I saw this in one of your dreams dear, the yellow towers rising from the depths of the rapids and the dark mouth opening ahead of me. Baby, it is perfect, exactly as you described it. Where are you taking me? Why am I following you?

There it is again, that damn hunger. I can smell the old remnants of salt flowing from their pores. I must, I must feed. I cannot control myself any longer. (Aaauughhhhhhh) It is unbearable! This pain is piercing my abdomen; it is killing me.

Look, over by that gate, I can sense two untainted souls cowering in the corner. Quick, I must compose myself; maybe I can blend in. But, this pain- this pain is killing me!

It is weird how the infestation has taken control of my body; yet, my mind remains sound (at least, for the most part). Amazingly, it seems as though I can manage these insatiable cravings; control them until the flesh calls to me, that aroma-the fragrance, the blood flowing like bitter gravy over your loins, I cannot take it any longer. I must; I must feast.

I am close now, about five feet from them. Honestly, I do not think they realize I am near. My sanity sets me apart from the monsters that are devouring the city. I can see my hand reach out and grab that tall blonde woman; her screams echo through the empty pathways and shake my soul as I grasp her tightly. Her partner turns while pulling the trigger of her cannon. Wait, no!

How can that be? The bullet tore through me. I can feel the shards taking hold in my insides, but I still stand here with the remains of her friend in my arms. Look the brains, now, the intestines; they are divine, absolutely divine! Her soft skin slides effortlessly across my lips, her veins aged to perfection; it is as if I have tasted her before.

Damn, as I turn to her friend, another bullet barely misses me. It is her turn to be my savior. That is unless she runs. Move damn it. I will not chase you; I am content with this beauty. I still have a few minutes before she turns and joins the quest. Run, please run, I promise I will not follow you; at least, not yet. (Click)

II

Insanity, these accounts are utter insanity. Incredibly, not only do I have more stories from where these early ones came from, and as impossible as it may sound, some of these people actually interacted with each other throughout their ordeal. That is the case with this next story I dug out of my notes (Thank God for cell phones, tablets, and the digital age- everything was recorded). I am starting this account here, as it appears that our lover boy and this group were close. Actually, it appears that many of these people are in the same vicinity, unless the name Ester is making a comeback (somehow, I do not see that in this twisted age). On with this story, ironically this chick, Morgan (from what I can decipher) had a chance to waste the fucker. Unfortunately, while she has the weapon of choice, her aim is a bit off...

Hurry up Esther; I do not see any of those monsters that have plagued our escape.

All I see is that homeless man over there and he looks helpless (and hopeless). Plus, now that I have my shotgun, we should be safe. I just wish I knew how to kill those bastards.

Hopefully, we can make it across the bridge and escape the city. Once we make it to the country, we will be safe. At least, that plan makes sense to me. You know, who would have thought that a couple of lesbians would have lasted. Maybe the rainbow is a bit misleading; maybe they should change that dreadful symbol to something more masculine.

Damn, did that man disappear? Esther, do you see him, where did he go? Never mind, just stay close to me and hold your emotions in check; we cannot afford another of your meltdowns. So please, for once, just maintain your focus for our future and us. When we survive, I promise all of our dreams will come true. Ester, hurry up you are scaring me.

I know you are tired, but be strong; we can make it. No, we will make it. I promise you. Nothing will happen to you as long as we are close. Besides, from the looks of it, there is no one left alive out there to fuck with us. Those demonic hoards must be full as well, as I still do not see or hear any those vile creatures around us.

Esther! Esther! Damn it; get your rotting hands off her. Esther, nooooo! Help me! Help us! Someone, anyone... Get off her before, before I blow you to hell and back. Fuck you then! Die you bastard!

Oh my god, that bullet, it, it, it didn't phase that monster. He would not stop; he just kept eating. I know that I did not miss; it had to shatter his rib cage. Oh God, no not her beautiful face, no! Her eyes, please, not her eyes. Stop it, you fiend! Oh, damn, I missed with that one. Esther, I am so sorry, I was supposed to protect you and guard you with my life. Now, I have failed. God Damn you- you festering beast, fuck you. I must escape; I must carry out our plans. Ester, your sacrifice must be for naught.

I love you!

Run, I have to run to the bridge. I must cross the Monongahela and reach the countryside; I have to get out of here. Damn, another one. What do I do? How can I kill them? Only seven bullets left, these beasts must have a flaw; they cannot be immortal. Nothing lasts forever! The head, yes, maybe the head.

III

What a small world we live in. That account reminds me of the time I was watching a Pittsburgh Steelers game in Fredericksburg, Virginia, and the person at the table next to us said, "you look familiar, are you from Pennsylvania?" Shocked because he did not look familiar to me, we started talking. Here, he knew my father when they were a little younger and I guess I have a small resemblance. Even more ironic is the fact that the town I grew up in is extremely insignificant and I was hundreds of miles away. One thing remained the same, though, the love of the Black and Gold and the love of Rolling Rock. Do not get me started on Rolling Rock; selling out to corporate America was a travesty, one that proved that even the most sacred institution is driven by greed.

Enough about me, there is more work to be done (a lot more). There are tons of passages in this notebook and on these recordings that need to find the light of day. Couple that with the fact that I am still motivated to work tonight, I may be able to put a dent in this text. With Esther apparently a feast, maybe the two damsels in the area will team up and escape the madness together; it does appear that our pregnant beauty is gaining on her (and the undead lover boy). Let us dive into the next account together and see where we end up.

February 14 (Continued),

Hold on, baby. I had to stop and take another break. We are almost through the tunnel. Once we make it through, we have about three miles before we can hopefully find the house I remember. With any luck, we will find safety and salvation there. Three miles may seem like a lot, but with what is happening, that is a drop in the bucket. I still cannot believe how Esther looked, the despair in her eyes. Strange though, she looked almost alive, baby, I have no idea how she could have survived that vicious attack.

As I look ahead, I can see some light. Eli, I think we are almost there. I am still worried about your father. Damn you, Isaac, why did you run off? Eli, if ever I needed him, it is now. He was supposed to protect us; at least, that is what he said in his vows. I guess it is my fault; I did entrust the most important bond on Earth to a stranger.

If I survive and ever find you a father, if a man even exists out there, I swear that the Lord, our Father, will preside over that union. I know I am not very religious, never have been, but these creatures have me praying and questioning everything I thought I knew. No, Eli, that is a lie; these creatures have me begging for forgiveness. I know I have sinned, but I meant well, I really did. I love you!

CHAPTER SEVEN

**"THEN I SAW AN ANGEL
COMING DOWN FROM HEAVEN..."**

OCTOBER 21

Damn it, and I was on such a roll last night until I was swept up into the emotion and feelings held within these accounts. Everyday that I venture into this world, I feel such an attachment to these victims, an attachment to the unbelievable atrocities that took place. Tyranny truly is a disease, as those bastard globalist pawns never had to answer for their deeds. In fact, to this day they deny any of this ever took place. But, it did and they will never be able to prevent these stories from getting out.

Where was I? Oh, yeah, the woman. I would love to learn that person's name. I have to find out what happened to her in the end. I can only hope that she, and her child, survived this ordeal. Honestly, no one deserves to fall prey to the unbearable evil when they have so much to live for.

Today is a new day though; I wonder where I should start. I guess it is time to dive back into the prophet. It has been a few days since I have experienced his sermon. I am a sinner and need to be absolved of my sins; maybe he would be available for confession. Who knows, maybe the Eucharist would help wash away these visions that overwhelm my being. I could possibly convert; his scripture does seem in line with a more modern way of thinking. Well, at least if you are undead.

I

On this day, a steel chariot will streak
across the Grand Confluence
Erupting with the force of Vesuvius and
the angels among you will weep
From the ashes, a golden triangle
will appear to the Messiah
Consecrating this fertile land as thy sacred sanctum
And the sinners among you will rejoice
in the Fountain of Forgiveness

(The Revelation of Moloch 2.13)

Look ahead my faithful; again, our lord speaks truths. The Fountain of Forgiveness lies at the confluence of the mighty rapids. Blessed be the name of the lord, for through his words our history comes to light. I can sense this is a momentous time for us. Our evil prey may have found a flaw in our perfection. We must remain vigilant in our proceedings, bearing true faith to the holy trinity at hand. Dark days for the festering vermin that desiccate our thoroughfares are near.

Again, I saw a vision of beauty from one of our herd. Her sinuous red hair flowing like the blood of the lone martyr, her heart pulsating with our sour wine, and her thighs opening the forbidden garden

for our satisfaction. Indeed, her pleas for pleasure will be answered. The signs of our mission lay before us, our righteous path designed by God. Let us go forth and continue his pilgrimage, and consign our redemption in his eyes. Let us cleanse this filthy world in his name
Let us pray.

Lord of Light
As we pursue our passage through purgatory
Guide us through the torment that
these vile sinners harbor
Forgive them for the misconceptions
created by their prophets
The words of the broken down blasphemers
whom you cast out of Eden
Forgive them for slandering your
gracious and holy name
For the insolence is not of their doing
You alone have the power to turn
their blood into wine
Give us the strength to complete this battle
in your name
To lead them through the temptations
scattered along their path
In your name, we pray
Amen

II

As the bishop continues to ready his congregation for the rapture, it seems as if our professors of stupidity are still making their way from the confines of their torture chamber. As I type this up, I cannot help but hope that they run into a group of hungry parasites. I am positive that they deserve to be the ones made into the latest Golden Corral. They started this shit with their illegal human experimentation; therefore, they warrant nothing more than to be a main course at the local raw bar. Unfortunately, from reading ahead, only one may fall this time.

(Play) The Boulevard at last, we have finally made it through the city; our salvation lies ahead. I think we are safe for the moment. At least, we are as safe as we can be in this plagued nightmare. We should stop and rest; there are no signs of those beasts anywhere and we will need all of our energy to make it out of the city. If my calculations are correct, we have about two miles until we hit the bridge and nine miles to our sanctuary.

We do not have long though. Our pheromones make us tempting entrées out here in the open. I still cannot believe how the immunization has mutated; it never should have caused this type of reaction. I swear we are living in some sort of butterfly effect. Damn, I wish I had brought a gun. Yes, these foul beasts can be can be killed at close range with a targeted blow to the head, but I would still prefer to distance myself from them. Are you about ready to move again?

Great, just in time. Look, over by the Console Energy Center, here they come. Damn, their senses are even better than I imagined. Amazing! It is incredible how the outbreak has spread so quickly through the population; there has to be 5000 or so packed into that small area (way too many for me to stand here and count, that's for sure). Time to move on; we must hurry.

Quickly, down this alley. I remember this from when I was a freshman at Duquesne. Yes, this should aid our escape. God, wrong turn! Damn it, those creatures are everywhere. How could they have surrounded us so quickly? It is almost as if they knew we were coming this way, like they knew our escape route. What to do, what to do? I guess, Paul?

Paul, stop, there are far too many for you to handle. We must take refuge. Look, that building would be perfect; the foundation is built on the shoreline. Maybe there is a boat in that shed down there we could find something to aid in our escape. Paul, get back here! Mark, John, head inside, Paul, please!

Stop it, Paul! Please! Please stop, I have enough blood on my hands from this experiment. I could not live with myself if I lost another. No! Over Here! No, leave him alone! It, It is me you want. Hey, over here! Damn you! Stop, oh God, what have I done? Paul, not you, you bastards want me! I did this; I created you. I built the lab and designed the vaccination. Take me! Here I am; yes, leave him alone. I deserve to die. Please lord, have them take me and not Paul, he is innocent.

That is the way, leave him alone. If only I had some type of weapon. Paul, run! Meet Mark and John in that building, and I will be right behind you. Run, run as fast as you can; they are listening, coming for me. Yes, Paul, that door! You are almost there, 20-yards and you will be safe! Ten more steps Paul, that is all, just ten more. Thank God...

No! Stop! No! Where did that abomination come from? You bastard! Get your mouth off him. Oh God, Paul, no. God, he is tearing into his neck, ripping at his flesh. Oh God, no, not Paul! **(Stop)**

That is fucked up; they ate the wrong one; so much for my thinking that they were actually intelligent. You know, I need to shut up before you;

the readers believe that I am a sympathizer for
these ungodly servants. No way, besides if I were,
would I donate my time to help the recovery of those
inflicted and injured during the tribulation? I would
not this so, but I do. In fact, I go down to the center
almost daily. Which reminds me, I have to run; I
have a meeting at the hospice. I will return and pick
the story up right here.

III

OK, I am back. When I left this afternoon, I never
expected that meeting to take quite as long as it
did. It is amazing how many people crawl out of the
woodwork when they discover that you are compiling
an account of government-sanctioned genocide
from this type of perspective. I guess everyone wants
his or her story to be heard. I took great notes. In
fact, I filled yet another notebook of material. It is
a shame, though; I think that the characters that I
am working with are perfect. There seems to be an
unnatural connection between them. Crazy, especially
considering that this whole ordeal is fucking cruel.
Where do I continue? I think I will dive back into the
story of our lovely lesbian. How outrageous, the world
is coming to an end and one of the main characters in
this true story is a damn lesbian wielding a shotgun.
Who says feminism is dead?

*Fuck yeah, direct hit! Die you bastard! The
head, it is definitely the head. That will stop these
monsters in their tracks. Damn, I wish I had more
ammunition, or at least, had this revelation before
now. If I would have known, I may have been able
to protect you, to save you like I promised.*

*Too late to be remorseful now, I must get
out of here before I end up on the wrong end*

of this outbreak. I want no part of becoming a bloodthirsty freak. I want to survive; to carry out the plans we discussed, even if I will be alone, even if I must spend my life without you.

The tunnel, I have to make it through the tunnel. I hope my path is somewhat clear; I cannot afford to battle many more of these beasts right now. I must find someplace safe, somewhere I can defend myself and pick and choose my targets wisely.

If I remember right, there is a cemetery. Yes, I must make it to the cemetery.

CHAPTER EIGHT

**"ONE OF THE FOUR BEASTS SINGS
COME AND SEE AND I SAW A
ND BEHOLD A WHITE HORSE..."**

OCTOBER 22

I cannot believe that I woke up with such a headache. It is funny, I do not even remember going to bed last night. From the look of it, I never made it off the couch. I guess I passed out from exhaustion; I have been working extremely hard on this project lately. What sucks is that I am quite motivated this morning, even with my headache. I wish I did not have to go to my therapy appointment, I actually believe I could make some great strides today once the Aleve sets in. Before I shower, let me knock a small part out though. I pulled this out last night before I went down. It appears that our lover boy, yeah that one, the one that does not realize he is a zombie is calling his beloved Gabrielle again.

I

(Click) *My angel, my savior, I still cannot fathom what has happened to me. Everything*

*is different now. Every taste richer, every
thought deeper, even every hour feels longer.
This revelation of clarity surrounds me; all of
my visions of betrayal replaced by you; fulfilling
every need, charging every emotion, and shaping
every impulse. I flutter at the thought of my
unyielding sense of bliss. Off in the horizon I can
feel you near, the togetherness we have dreamt
finally at hand*

*Why do I long to hold you so? Where are you? At
times, the feelings overwhelm my senses. Burning
tears swell in my eyes, their bitterness inflaming
past wounds and opening a pathway to my soul.
My heart cries out for your flesh, longing to spend
an eternity in your arms; your sweet nectar
vanquishing the demons that haunt me; erasing
the victims of my merciless behavior.*

*Thoughts of you differ, though, my vicious ego in
limbo; my sadness a distant memory suppressed
by your breath. Are you a messenger from above, a
saint in disguise?*

*An equal? Your presence challenges every
endeavor, quenches every thirst. My heart
held at the crossroad by your perfection, your
understanding of every thought. I know I had loved
before, cared, and even nurtured before. Yet, this
yearning, this craving is different, your fruit more
tempting than the vine.*

*I can taste you still; the familiarity is frightening,
your aromatic bouquet fresh on my lips, your
enticing skin warm in my hands. However, I
cannot remember our last embrace or our last
real kiss. When was the last time I lay at your
breast? Have we actually shared the intimacy that
I perceive?*

Strange, how my mind works now. My ideals, my perspectives circling your beauty, although, your description still escapes me. I am lost without you. This complete emptiness overshadowing the world I held sacred. Now, I am destined to devour everything in my path until I can hold you again, until we can grow, or until our family can grow together.

I know that you will be the perfect mother to my son. Your essence alone is evidence enough, illuminating the endless possibilities of happiness that exist in your heart. I can almost see the many nights of redemption in your bed. Where are you darling? Gabrielle? Why have you forsaken me? Please return to my side, so we can become one and open the door to dine upon our neighbor's splendor.

You too can enjoy their divine intelligence, their mouthwatering wine. Come to me, let me share with you the pleasures of indulging yourself on the purity of their bosom; sipping their milk until they run dry, and harvesting the spirit that failed them. In reality, their messiah that left them cold and alone. Only together can we complete their marvelous transition. Only together, can we survive this nightmare. **(Click)**

II

The words he used, my angel, those are powerful and heartfelt, that had to be genuine and everlasting love. I had an angel once, she was a picture of beauty, and more importantly, she kept me balanced. When I woke every day, I wanted to share every breath, every thought. Unfortunately, all I have left is a few picture scattered around this apartment, as I lost her during this plague. The infestation that ravaged society tore her apart, and she was taken from me. Where she went, or what exactly happened to her, I have no idea, but I have searched. For days, weeks, and months, I searched for her. In many ways, I am still searching, and this book, this project is keeping her alive in my heart.

Damn, my head. This fucking headache has to go. Maybe I should just lay down, and possibly take a nap.

CHAPTER NINE

**"I REBUKE AND PUNISH
ALL WHOM I LOVE..."**

OCTOBER 23

I am truly sorry about that; I just could not take the pain anymore. The sound was deafening, my pulse echoing through my head. And the screams, I could hear the scream from my nightmares torturing me as I sat there looking over my notes, listening to the tapes, I wanted it to end, I want it to go away.

Unfortunately, these are some of the side effects from the medications that the doctors have prescribed. Fucking bastards are probably poisoning me, the same way they murdered the innocents during the outbreak. Yes, the CDC and WHO have been closed because of the illegal and unethical eugenics they were practicing, but we must stay vigilant to prevent the next group from rising. These fascist technocrats and their globalist ideologies are always trying rise up and destroy freedoms. They always have.

Where do I go from here? My entry yesterday was so alive and full of emotion; it will be hard to follow. I know, I will get back to our expecting mother and see how she is holding up in this untamed world.

I

February 14 (continued),

I can't believe how exhausted I am, between the distance and you inside me, I can barely function. I need to find us some shelter soon. I know stopping was a risk, but the road to the cemetery is in sight! Thank God for that, he is definitely watching over us tonight. If I remember correctly, that house I have written about is just across the cemetery. The last time I was up here, I thought is was empty. Maybe it is abandoned. Come to think about it, I have never seen anyone there and I think it is boarded up.

I am just thankful that those things slacked off. I wish I knew what was really happening out there; it is insane. Eli, my words in this journal can't do this ordeal the justice it deserves. When you get older, you will understand the surrealistic visions, I mean, there are no cars. When you read this, let that sink in for a second, the roads are empty. Empty, why, we cannot be the only ones that have survived to this point. There have to be others out there; besides, I need someone to help me take care of you.

Wow, I have been so panic struck that I did not think of that at all. What am I to do if I go into labor? Who will help with the delivery? Damn, I hope there is someone around. I changed my mind; I want someone at that house as long as it isn't one of those loathsome strangers that have driven us this far. This may sound crazy, but I feel like Little Red Riding Hood hiding from the wolf. In this case, I hope that the wolf has not already eaten grandma.

In time, I will tell you all of those nursery rhymes. I will start when we get to the house. I may have to buy a book. though, or maybe, download one, or buy one on CD. I will be honest with you; I suck at nursery rhymes. Not your dad, he knows them all by heart. Damn him, where is he when I need him?

Alright, I am almost ready to go again and it looks as if we are in luck, the cemetery gates are open. We can cut through here and make it to the house faster. It looks like we will be able to relax in no time. Once we get there, I promise, I will tell you one of those rhymes. Which one would you like to hear? Humpty Dumpty? I hope that one works, I think I know all of the words. If not, I can at least make something up. Hold on; I love you!

II

Incredible, such resolve in the face of devastation. To think that she is pregnant, and can stand alone in the face of these vile creatures, while protecting her unborn child. If only everyone could be that strong or that resilient in the face of adversity. Maybe if more people had that type of strength, this nightmare would have never taken place.

Of course, all of these accounts are not centered on love or even survival. Some accounts definitely have tones that are more sinister. Personally, I cannot for the life of me understand the meaning of the religious leader, why is he here, what does he want, where did he come from? All I know is that his preaching upon the mount is organizing the infected faster than they can be defeated.

The Almighty spoke and the earth trembled
Thou shall drive the infidels into the
Chasm of Flame
Their sins cleansed at the hand of the father
The Great Beast opened his mouth at
the base of the mount
And laughed at their despair

(The Revelation of Moloch 3.13)

My children, my flock, behold the mighty beast, his teeth glistening in sunlight, waiting for our offering. At last, the purification of the heretics is at hand. We must show them the light, the way of our Father.

Look, there are three nonbelievers at the mouth. Look at their disregard for the Great Beast. Praise god for allowing us the ability to watch their refinement; to see them repent at the hand of the Father. Their deliverance lies before them. Praise be, as our Lord has prophesized, our congregation will grow.

Soon, we shall discover more sinners awaiting baptism along our path. Their wills' broken by the deception of faith. We must rise up and show them the way to eternal glory. We must lead them to the forgiveness of their original sin, to share the flesh and blood of our father, the host of redemption. Let us pray.

Lord of Light
We saw three sinners cross our path
in search of liberation

Their actions unkind, yet, they wait for
deliverance from the grand plague
Give us the strength to lead them into the garden
The vigor to dine on the fruit
Absolving their damnation for eternity
They know not of your high and holy name
Nor the legend of your might
Pardon them from their abstinence and misdeeds
Give them the purity of your forgiveness
The salvation they seek
In your name, we pray
Amen

III

I am still having trouble wrapping my head around the fact that the infected had a majority of their minds left intact. Every time I dive into the religious ramblings, I cannot help but be amazed at the focus, and message. It is incredible how his scriptures mirrored the landscape and events. You have no idea how much I would love to get my hands on a copy of his bible, or at least a journal of his prayers.

As I think about it now, it should be no surprise that an alternate religion seemed to rise from the ashes during this outbreak. With the constant attack on Christians, the blind support for radical Islam, and the desire of the New World Order to create a one-world religion, it would make sense. Hell, even the Catholics had issues, as their newly elected liberal pope has sent many of the most devout bishops into a death spiral with his once considered heretical thoughts rising to the forefront of his teachings.

Well, enough about that. Are you cold? It is freezing in here and those random voices that have infiltrated my mind have started screaming again. I can almost feel their pain as these screams creep into my soul. I wonder if that is what it felt like being on the road fighting for your life. I wonder if that is what our lesbian with a shotgun was feeling as she made her way through the tunnel.

I am half way through the tunnel and there is not a monster in sight. So far, this has been easier than I expected, yet, I keep hearing sounds coming from behind me. Why are they still following me? Damn, I am exhausted, I need to stop, and I need a break. At least they are not in front of me; I swear I have no energy to take on that army of undead and it seems like they are everywhere.

Where are all of the people, especially the fucking police? Those damn bastards are never around unless they are conducting an illegal checkpoint to infringe on my liberties. I swear I cannot be the only one left. Let me tell you; there is no way I intend on spending my life alone, especially on the god-forsaken planet. At this point, I think I would be better off on Mars. At least, those life forms are not cannibals like these creatures. God, wh-wh-what is that smell, that rot?

From the looks (and smell) of it, they have already been through here. The devastation is just like that of the city, everything torn to shreds. Funny, I do not see any remains either. I wonder, no, they cannot be regenerating. Nothing has the capacity to come back to life. Am I wrong? God, I hope that I am wrong.

Fuck that would mean, no, not my beautiful Esther. She cannot. There was, was nothing

*left to her. That inhuman scum was devouring
her intestines, mutilating her soft skin; he was
devouring her lovely face. Her eyes, I can still see
the despair in her eyes, what torture, and torment.
I swear I am going to fuck them all over as soon as
I can find a safe haven. I am going to do whatever I
have to do to make these pieces of shit burn in Hell.
Not just for you dear, but for all of the innocents that
have been caught in their web. Finally, the light,
there is the light. Wait, what is that, footsteps? I
must hurry to the light; hose sounds are closing in.*

IV

Jeez, look at the time. I cannot believe how late
it is getting. Honestly, it feels as if I just sat down
at this computer to get some work done. Even
after this time trying to become a writer, I am
still amazed at how fast time moves when I am
immersed in this world. Everything would be
perfect if I didn't become one with the stories. I can
feel the emotions, smell the decomposed flesh of
the victims, and even hear their screams. Those are
the worst, the screams, and once they start, they do
not go away. Please, God, make them stop, I cannot
take them anymore.

Damn, it is late. I should go to bed; I am
exhausted. 9:57, I must get some sleep. No, not yet,
I have one more account set out for tonight and I
must finish it. I cannot be weak, as the weakness
got our beloved nation into this ordeal in the first
place. Had we stood up against the tyrants early on,
and spoke the truths that lay before us, maybe this
despicable disease would have stayed in the lab.
Unfortunately, it did not, and ironically, it became
the spark that started this mass awakening that is

taking place today. With that in mind, now would be the perfect time to check in on those responsible for out dilemma. Maybe another one will get the treatment they deserve.

(Play) Damn it Paul, why? Mark, John, please be careful, I cannot lose another. My heart can only take so much of this devastation. You know, Paul was like a brother to me. He challenged me to take risks, to rise above the data. Regrettably, those challenges may have sit at the heart of this plague. Please, guys, stay safe; knowing this outbreak is my fault is punishment enough. I do not need to witness any more destruction.

Finally, the tunnel, we are almost safe. We do not have long, though, and cannot afford to take much time regrouping. Look, over there. Across the bridge, a large mass of those creatures appears ready to pounce. Damn it, what have I done? From the look of it, we have little time to catch our breath, and we must keep moving through the tunnel.

I wonder who that was that was in front of us; I wonder where they are going. At least that makes four of us that have survived this massacre. Incredible, four humans are unaffected, that is impossible, there has to be more. At least, I hope that was human, it could just be us; I did not get a great look at the other one.

Fuck, here they come, run! Damn it, I am too old for this shit and cannot take much more. It reminds me of days on that research vessel in the Persian Gulf where we would run twice a year because of some stupid policy. That shit does not seem so senseless now; I wish I were still working out.

Focus, I must focus. The data I have here has to provide an answer. Where did I go wrong with that vaccine? What triggered this rapid change in our subjects? Flesh, why the flesh? I wonder...
(Stop)

CHAPTER TEN

**"NOW HIS MESSIAH HAS
SHOWN HIS AUTHORITY..."**

OCTOBER 24

Stop, please stop, these voices, these screams are
destroying me. It has to be the stress, and the
doctors warned if I did not stop working on this
project; I would go insane. Hell, I am already there,
why stop now? You know, insanity does run in the
family. I remember my grandmother; she was not
right at all. She used to talk all the time about the
"outbreak" and how that beautiful blonde girl was
attacked in the cemetery. I always thought she was
talking about *Night of the Living Dead*, but who
knows, maybe this has happened before.

Shut up! What the fuck do you want? Why won't
you leave me alone? Those damn cries again, I
wish I knew where they were coming from. That
way I could just tell them in person to shut the
fuck up. Or better yet, make them shut up. Thank
you! Now, where was I? Oh yes, that badass chick
that annihilates everything in her path. I like her.

She reminds me of someone I was once close to. I wonder where she is at, could she have survived. The last I heard from her she was battling cancer. Oh well, it is probably better if I don't know.

I

Finally, the end of the tubes, at last, I never thought that tunnel would seem so long. Even when I was stuck in traffic inside it always seemed so peaceful; the darkness always made me feel at home. Now, I fear the darkness for what it may bring tonight. If I do not find shelter soon, I may not survive until morning.

There it is again. That smell, that overwhelming fragrance of rot! Those footsteps are gaining ground; I can almost hear them breathing. Thankfully, it is still daylight; I think that I can make a few more miles before I have to stop, although I think I could.

I still cannot believe you are gone. All of the plans and all of our dreams, Esther, I will always love you. Even if I eventually have to make you look like your idol, you know, John F. Kennedy. Ironic, I never thought you would live that Jesus and Mary Chain song. You know the one, Blown away on a sunny day, what was that songs name?

Damn it! Why I can't remember that songs name?

Why? I'll tell you why. I was such a miserable partner. You deserved better than me. You deserved someone who could have protected you. I knew I should have paid more attention to your likes. No, I should have paid more attention to you. You are my world. No, you are everything.

Fuck, I hate this. I hate those vile beasts that feasted on you; that destroyed our future. I

swear to you, Esther, I will kill as many as those
motherfuckers as I can. They will pay for this pain,
for your death. If it is the last this I do, I swear,
they will pay for destroying our lives.

Reverence, I think that is it. Yeah, it was
Reverence,

II

Every time I start to dive into her words, I can feel
the pain. She must have loved Esther more than
anyone could ever imagine. I knew love like that
once, but that was many years ago before this plague
of destruction tainted out soil. Now, who would love
me? Who would deal with me, and the splintered
reality that I live in? My thoughts exactly, now,
where was I?

Oh yes, our pilgrimage with the religious one
(and people tell me that I am crazy). This one keeps
getting stranger every time I break into his verse.
Honestly, I have no idea what to expect when I
start unveiling his words. It is hard to believe that
his words could organize this horde so quickly. If
someone could discover his secret, the world would
be in trouble.

The mass heard God profess his wisdom to his son
Behold, the great journey through
damnation lies ahead
Lead your minion through the Mouth
of Hecate to the solemn grotto
There, surrounded by fern and oak,
her mighty gate has opened
And the chosen one awaits your entrance

(The Revelation of Moloch 7.4)

Listen to the sinners disperse, their pulse betraying their desires, their scent drawing us near. Do you hear another banquet calling to us? Indeed, it anticipates us. Come, follow me, before we reach the meadow, our congregation must partake in this communion.

Mighty Melek Taus, thank you for enlightening our journey and opening your mouth to reveal the path of righteousness. Did you leave the malefactors for us? Or did you devour them for desecrating your sanctity? Protect us as we pass through your depths, the search for the prophesized one leads us this way. Our journey to Mecca nears an end. Only there, may our faithful providence be revealed.

Through the horizon, I can sense another amongst the serpents. Can you feel him? His young heart calls to me for salvation and the cravings flowing through his veins are high. Hmmm, his baptism upon the embers of darkness has been foretold. Unborn, yet already in league with our father, yes, the fabled apostle will ascend to the throne. At last, our mighty general will rise from his refuge and show us the way to salvation.

Let us pray.

Lord of Light
Give us the strength to continue our mission
Help us enlighten the non-believers with your gospel
Leading them to the fruits of indulgence
upon your tree
We bow before thee, alone,
preparing for communion
Waiting to rise as one, in thy name
Ignite the eternal flame of power for us to follow
As we maneuver through this

unforgiving wasteland
Thy prophecy at hand
In your name, we pray
Amen

III

Ironically, when I venture into the religious aspects of this crazy outbreak, I feel overwhelmed by some emotion. I can't explain it; every passing word, and syllable draws me into the ordeal again and makes me want to profess all of my sins. It's funny, yesterday when I was battling another one of those headaches from the phantom screams that echo through my apartment, I felt the warmth of his gospel as I thought about the words and their meanings.

What, sorry, something just shut up! Please, I beg of you stop, please. I can't take it anymore, who are you? Why won't you leave me alone? Please, shut the hell up.

(Click) *The warmth from the light in front calls to me; your splendor lay ahead.*

I can feel you near me, and I know I am closing our distance with every step, with every breath. Gabrielle, is that your name angel? Are you the one crying out for my touch, my embrace?

I believe that the other is following you as well. I can still smell her scent. Her aura surrounds me; devours my senses as you consume my mind. It is you; I crave with all my heart? It is you, who will make me whole, alive, to face eternity and share forever? There, in the shadows, I can see her. Amazingly, he calm demeanor transcends the panic. What vigor she must possess. Her brain must be delicious, her sacred font oozing with delight. I

*need to taste her; I must dine on her blessed loins
and sip from her rosy fountain.*

*Don't worry love it will only be dinner. I could
never share my bed with another. It is strange, but
somehow and someway, we share what seems to be
a permanent bond; energy so strong, so pure, I can
feel it liven my veins when my mind embraces you.
This relationship erases every doubt that clouds
my reality. Gabrielle, I long to hold you for the first
time, I savor the bitterness of your neck and the
tenderness in your kiss. Gabrielle, please give me
a sign. I beg of you, please, I must find you. I must
consummate this unyielding passion and fulfill all
of our dreams.* **(Click)**

IV

I'm so sorry for the abrupt disappearance earlier,
but those noises were becoming too much. Plus,
it did give me a chance to try out some of the new
software I was able to acquire during my last trip
to the clinic. It's amazing how willing they are to
help now when they and their sorry ass minions
were nowhere to be found during the outbreak (I
hope that underground bunker treated you well-
bastards). Damn government scum, maybe someday
karma will return the favor when the aliens arrive
and send a probe so far up their ass-- Damn, sorry, I
have to calm down before a headache comes back.

Where were we? Ahhh yes, we were just leaving
our tainted lover, who seems to be embracing his
new found craving for flesh. *"Savor the bitterness
in your neck,"* I appreciate his thoughts, but I could
think of many other things that I desire. Oh well, I
guess it is time to get back to the swine that started
this mess, those clueless scientists. One can only

hope that they meet their demise at some point.

(Play) *I can't believe how empty the tunnel is right now, where did they all go? I know we aren't alone, I can hear those beasts behind us. At least they are not surrounding us and hampering our escape. At this pace, we should make it to the cottage by dusk. Good thing too, I need a break; I need to scour these notes for answers. I know the secret has to be inside. These records will tell me where I went wrong.*

Come, we must hurry; the opening at the end is becoming more visible with every step. We do not have much further in here-15, 20 minutes maximum. Thank God, part of the nightmare is almost over. Mark, John, please keep moving. Whatever you do, do not look back; we must focus all of our attention on the light at the end of the tunnel.

Wait hang on a minute. Look up there at the mouth of the tunnel, is that? Yes, it has to be, there's a man, but no, it can't be. He looks like one of those vile beasts, yet he is alone. So far, I have only seen them amass, and hunt in packs. Could they be mutating already? Could the virus be smarter than I ever expected? I wonder. No, it can't be, I must be over tired and hallucinating. He couldn't be. **(Stop)**

**CHAPTER
ELEVEN**

**"AND THE EARTH HAS BEEN MADE DRUNK
WITH THE WINE OF HER FORNICATION..."**

OCTOBER 25

Can you just go away, please, just shut up and leave me alone! My fractured sanity cannot handle much more, and I just want the screams and shrieks to stop. I swear I am doing all I can to help bring down the shadow establishment that destroyed our city and our lives. I may be struggling to focus on this project, but I am trying my best to tell your story. I want nothing more than to expose the dark truth of what happened here for the entire world to see. I want everyone to understand the way they treated you and how all of you suffered at their hands, I am revealing the important details so these globalist bastards can't get away with it again.

I need Natalie to visit me right now and drive away these voices. She is the only person that has been able to silence them when they appear. I hate the fact that having any lasting relationship with Natalie is only a dream. I have flirted with her, and she continually laughs it off. There is no way someone as beautiful and smart as Natalie would ever want to spend quality time with someone as damaged as I. She's perfect, and I am nowhere near the type of man she would want in her life.

Look at the time; there is no way I am going to finish anything tonight. I wanted to dive back into our journeys and see what our different characters were up to, but your persistent cries have ruined that goal. What I need to do is try to get some sleep. All I know is that something has to give; your screams have been tormenting me for the past week, and I cannot take much more of them. I'm exhausted, and if I don't get some quality rest soon, I will collapse.

Renae that can't be you; that fervent moan echoing through the brisk night sky sounds exactly as I remember. I swear I can hear your scream drowning out the others inside my head, but I know there is no way that can be you; those murderous bastards stole you from me. I'm so sorry for not protecting you. I love you, and I still can't forgive myself for letting them take you and feast upon your flesh. I should have been here watching over you.

Dammit, maybe I should break down and just ask Natalie to dinner. Honestly, what do I have to lose? I lost everything I ever cared about when I lost you, Renae. Now, I am left with only a few pictures of your beauty and the lingering nightmares of those beasts overwhelming your soul. I bet your intestines tasted so sweet upon their lips, almost as mouthwatering as the memories of your inner thighs.

Oh God! What am I saying; what have I become?

CHAPTER TWELVE

"WHEN I SAW HER I WAS COMPLETELY AMAZED…"

OCTOBER 27

I'm so sorry for not being around over the past few days to continue documenting this tragedy. Those screams and voices in my head wouldn't stop, and I couldn't take it anymore. I decided to head to the clinic to see if there was anything they could do. They gave me some new (most likely experimental) drug designed specifically for this type anguish. Yes, it worked; the voices are gone. But, unfortunately, it made me so lethargic that I don't want to do anything except lay here and stare at the television.

I had to force myself off the couch and head over to the desk to try to get some work accomplished on this project. This story must be told, and I must be the messenger. It has been far too long in this country since the media outlets served the interests of the population. That damn elect in 2016 proved that. Mainstream media is nothing but a political arm for the unrighteous and corrupt politicians that pimped our country out to the highest bidder. Fucking United Nation globalist pigs.

Yeah, "*America Will Lead Again*," fuck that. We would still be great if these degenerates hadn't sold us into one-world slavery under the guise of safety. Caliphate, my ass; that piece of shit Scotereo spawned ISIS with his Muslim Brotherhood cronies and the funding of Spoos, Gales, and the Crentin Foundation. Fuck them all. I hope the plagued hosts violated them inside their secure bunker (none of them have been seen since the outbreak); I am sure that their brains would have tasted like sweeter than the spiritual fruit upon the tree of knowledge.

Damn, what am I saying, where did those words come from? Maybe this project is destroying me. That is what the doctor said before he gave me the prescription, *"Son, stop torturing yourself, this will do nothing except for keeping you psychological wounds fresh and open."*

Well sir, I totally disagree. If I don't document these events, who will? The majority of society has been brainwashed into the collective. They are convinced nothing happened. It's like 9-11. No one remembers that WTC Building 7 was not hit by a plane, and was nowhere near the fires (not to mention the BBC report that they were going to destroy the building for 'security" reasons). No, it is just part of the myth that was created to push the globalist agenda that had been searching for an enemy since the end of the Cold War.

Oh, sorry, sorry, I don't mean to be babbling to you. 9-11 is just one of those topics that grate on me. I still can't believe no one has ever sent in a request for the Emergency Locator Transmitter Data (ELT Data) from the planes, which could be a smoking gun. Of course, not as big as the 28 redacted pages from the 9-11 Commission report, but I digress. Damn, there I go ranting again, I should be working on the manuscript. Telling the stories that must be told. Now, where was I? Yes, that's it; I was with our mother-to-be and her child. I wonder how she is holding up?

I

February 14 (continued),

Baby, please hold on. I know this entire ordeal; the anguish has to be taking a toll on you. I can feel your kicks and your jabs, but honey, I can't stop running. We have come so far on this horrific journey, but still, we must push forward, we must survive.

Now that we are here wandering through this plain of the surreal, we must remain vigilant. There are so many unknowns around every corner; we have to make it through this cemetery.

So much has happened to us during this ordeal, I feel we are beyond words now, beyond actions. It is strange; it's not your hands that hold me. It's your soul, your mind. Even inside my womb, I can sense them calling out to me, keeping me here, focused on keeping you safe. You are as much a part of me as I am; you are inside me as no other has been before; as no other ever could before. I need your presence, I need to keep you safe and continue feeling you inside me.

With every step, my heart, and my passion— Every fervent desire is to survive. And, you drive all of these feelings, the feelings you have found, and the thoughts, which expose my darkest fears. Everything leaves little room for actions or words. I need neither because I can feel you. I feel the breadth of you inside me where you fill me with love. I feel your life echoing through my bounds where you can empty my every thought.

Sorry, we must stay focused here in the place where nothing is, as it seems. We must be resilient; one of those bastards may lay behind any stone or any tree. Their vile make-up is wanting nothing more than to tear you away from me and to devour your virgin flesh. With every step, I must protect you; we must make it to that house. I am sure we will find help there.

If only your father were here, I am positive he would take care of us. He always knew exactly what to do when things got rough. I know he would lead us to paradise where our lives would be too good to be true, much different from this dominion where Lucifer reigns at the edge of reality, where words mean nothing and actions less.

Incredibly, we seem to be the only ones out here. Are we the only survivors of this plague? Were we the only ones to escape the city and get away from these monsters?

I sure hope we find others out here surviving to see the dawn. I love you, baby, please hold on.

CHAPTER THIRTEEN

"THE FIRST HEAVEN AND FIRST EARTH DISAPPEARED..."

OCTOBER 28

Damn, it feels like forever since I sat at this computer to get back into documenting the apocalyptic nightmare that almost destroyed the Republic. It's hard to believe that last night I sat in this exact seat and went through an account of our pregnant maiden. Honestly, it feels like it has been weeks, maybe months since I sat here. It has to be that fucking medication from the clinic. Those bastards wanted me to give this up. Well, I have a surprise for them (and the globalist assholes that are funding them that is not going to happen. I won't stop! I can't stop!

Where was I? The maiden. Hmmm, where should I go from there? I have so much more to get to, the stacks of information, the words, the voices, haunt me like a forgotten tattoo carved into my flesh and sealed by the tainted blood of the lost souls that were destroyed by this plague.

Speaking of diseases, maybe that is the place

to start tonight. Our religious leader, he always has some prophetic and inspiration words in his sermons. Maybe we should focus on finding leaders such as him to lead our nation instead of the crap the election brought us in 2016. Crentin and Alexander, what the fuck is that? And to think that Trump is the lesser of two evils, unbelievable, truly unbelievable!

I

...And the Father spoke to the prophet
Beyond the crossroad of life lies a
dominion lined with markers of antiquity
Pass forth through the lost generations
to the derelict manger
Your arrival has been foretold
(The Revelation of Moloch 7.9)

Indeed, behold, the sinners persist; they continue to infect the corridors with their sinful behaviors. Their bodies reflect not the purity our father created in his image, but decadence sated with sin. The time is now, branch out and seize the infidels; feast upon their raw flesh, and harvest their viscera to fill our chalices with the bitter wine from their veins. Forgive them in the name of our Father, our most holy and everlasting Creator, for they were born into evil and knew nothing about the sanctity of thy Fathers' fruit.

For this, and for our salvation, we must give these degenerates their penitence. I know that they have forsaken his glory-forsaken us, but we must make them understand that he is the way of light and the holiest angel in the universe. With every bite, bless them; purify our host before cleansing their sins.

I forewarn you; this will not be easy. Many of your brothers will fall at the hands of these sinners, their armor is strong, and their faith will not waver. Stay resilient in the face of their deceit, as they will not fall willingly. Prey on their weakness, their guilt; let the power of the almighty guide you. Transform these creatures to our divine path and open their hearts in time to receive absolution.

We must be precise with our message. The Sands of Jericho continue to fall freely, and the fruit of our pilgrimage awaits our greeting. I can feel his heartbeat quicken with every step, with every breath. Our redemption is near; for the prophesized birth of Fathers' reincarnate is near.
Let us pray.

Lord of Light
Provide us with the wisdom to remain
steadfast in our hour of need
To maintain focus on your mission
Our enemy is strong
But, the light from your darkness encompasses all
Provide them with the warmth of your breath
And the eternal salvation of your Kingdom
In your name, we pray
Amen

II

I still can't believe how powerful those verses are. For some reason, his words seem to touch me in the same way that some of the great speeches from history continue to resonate in my soul. Powerful, thought provoking, meaningful, this man in his blue and white robe makes me wonder if there is a right or wrong side. I know that may sound crazy considering who he was, and the atrocities he called for, but it is the truth, and that is why we are here, to outline the truth.

Of course, we can't discuss the truth unless we revisit the man who may be guilty of creating these beasts (at least in his eyes), our scientist, and his friends. Honestly, the further I dive into these accounts, it is hard for me to hold this many solely responsible. If fact, the deeper I go, the more I see that our government and the legion of globalists that control them are the real enemies. Just look at the way they fought back when the truth started to funnel out. Hell, the election protests, the women's marches, everything was funded by the global dictatorship because society began to break from their spell.

Where were we, oh yes, the scientist? It's truly difficult sometimes to remember where exactly I was at with this project, between the medication, the nightmares, and the screams, I lose track. Oh yeah, they were in the tunnel.

(Play) Oh God, the army of undead approach. What have I done? Come on guys, run! If we don't, there is no hope for us. No, fuck, John, what are you doing! Stop, what the, stop, hurry up, you cannot defeat them. There are too many of them out here. Our only hope is to run. We must continue, we must find shelter. There, if we are lucky, I may be able to find some hint to what is causing this crazy infestation. Maybe we can discover an antidote for this festering rot. Please, we must find our, I mean, my mistake.

Stop, come on guys, haven't we lost enough already? Hasn't enough blood been shed? Hurry up! Mark, grab that rock, and aim for their fucking heads; I will act as a decoy. Hey, dumbass, over here you pieces of shit, it's me want. I am the one; I did this-I created you. Get away from him; he's innocent. John, fuck! Mark; hurry, oh God, no. Look at the pain, look at his suffering. They are, no; they can't be, they are tearing through his flesh. Look what they are doing to his skull; they are shredding it like paper. Wait, what, they seem to be sharing him, no, they can't be.

Oh God, what have I done? These vile beasts are sharing him. It looks like a mass. Look at the way they've surrounded him. They embraced him, all the while gashing his flesh and feasting on his bloodied corpse. Fuck! Are those creatures drinking his blood? It can't be. These maggot lovers are fucking devouring him. Stop! Enough already, you want me!

Damn it to Hell, these fiends must be destroyed, and all of these deaths must be avenged. Mark, Mark, we have to press on through the tunnel. We must survive this ordeal. I believe that the cemetery gates are just ahead once we exit this deathtrap; once there, we should be home free. Mark, are you listening to me? Promise me you will listen; promise me you will survive with me to find a cure. Mark, please, help locate the mistake. You are all that I have left on this Earth; you are my only family now.

I know this may be hard; after all, everything I have touched has been poisoned or destroyed. I'm not evil. I am sure there is an explanation. All I know is that I have nothing. I have nobody. All I have left is my work. Honestly, there is nothing more to drive me. How good is that? Its pathetic isn't it? I deserve this fate. I do, I am a monster. I am just like those abominations, I stand here lost and alone feasting on the meek. I'm sorry Mark, but, this scene speaks volumes; I am a murderer! (Stop)

III

Wow, still in the tunnel, I was sure they would have made it through by now. I have been through those tubes many times in my car, but never on foot. I couldn't imagine what it would be like in the darkness fighting for your life. It has to feel like an eternity inside. I am sure that we will hear more from these scientists again sooner rather than later.

While these men are busy attempting to escape the city to find solitude somewhere, one of the others is still searching for his distant lover. Looking back now, it is interesting that the virus that ravaged his flesh allowed him to think, and maintain the memories he held dear. Unfortunately, that doesn't seem to be the results of many of the pharmaceuticals today, many not only ravage the body; they devastate the mind. I know that the shit they have me on makes me feel dead inside, and the pain from the side effects is unbearable. At least, I am alive (that is one of the harsher ones).

Enough about that, though, it is just a relief that the VA doctors moved on from Motrin. Now, where were we? Yes, we were with our man searching for Gabrielle. I wonder how close they are. He did say he could sense her.

(Click) Gabrielle, darling Gabrielle, where are you dear? Why aren't you here in my arms? My heart races at the mere thought of holding you and finally completing the unholy bond we share. You do realize that we are meant to be. We are destined

to share one soul and have our pulse echoing
through the night. Our one love spanning eternity

With every step I take, you are here. Your warm
tears call me to the passion burning deep within
your loins. I can tell that you are waiting for my
touch to soothe your every pain and wipe the sorrow
from your pale beauty. I can feel it with every step
and taste it with every breath. Over the horizon, I
can see you still. Are you still searching for a savior?
Let me be the one, crucify me with your anguish.

Damn it, what's that; it has to be, the other is
near. I can smell her. That scent, with every step
that musky aroma haunts me. Ever since my affair
with that street walking whore earlier tonight, that
fragrance has overtaken my senses when we are
near. I must have her as well. Where is she? Is she as
delicious? Hmmm, that thought alone moistens my
lips; I can almost taste her.

If she is anything like her friend, I know she will
taste divine. She has to. Her thighs, her mouth, her
brains; it will be a feast set for a king. Now, I just
have to find her.

Where is she hiding? I must have her, taste her. I
must satisfy her! (Click)

IV

Sorry that I cut that one off so abruptly, I can't
stop crying. Why am I crying? Those words, those
feelings. Yeah, I remember when I had feelings
like that. It has been a long time. Especially now,
with the way society has spiraled out of control.
Things were supposed to get better once that dunce
Scotereo started to transition out of office, but
in many ways, they got worse. Sure, the globalist

agenda was stopped, but the damage was already done. It seems like everyone was radicalized. Brother against brother, friend against friend, no one was safe.

As I have mentioned many times in this manuscript (probably too many), that is why I am fighting through this project and ensuring these accounts get out. Citizens of the world must hear these accounts, and they must realize that none of us are safe in this world. Those bastard global elites will stop at nothing to have their planned world domination agenda forced on the population.

I know, I know, these are, but words on paper and many will call it a work of fiction instead of the truth. However, if just one person reads this, believes it and passes it on, maybe, just maybe it can start waking some of the blind to the reality that we all face. After all, it may have taken decades, but Orwell's classic 1984 again became a best seller (much deserved and a must read book).

All right, back to the script. Where should we go? Maybe this would be a good time to see where "the other one" mentioned above is at. Our man believes she is close. Is he right?

Damn it, Esther I need you. I will always need you. Please, help lead me through this abyss, help me escape this misery. Look, over there, is that the bastard that ripped my heart out and stole you from my grasp? It damn sure looks like him! I swear I want nothing more than to bring vengeance and to erase every sign of his existence. I wish I, fuck, what is that?

I have to keep moving. I cannot afford to do battle right now. Plus, I have this strange sensation, this weird feeling inside of me. Something, or yes, someone is calling me. They need my help. Looking around this now desolate town, I think I am the only other one alive out here. I know that can't be true, there are too many of us for no one else to survive, but right here, right now that feels like the case. Why here, though, a cemetery, damn I hate cemeteries; they always gave me the creeps.

Well, until the next time I can talk to you, please remember that black bird on the tombstone. The one you chased around for three hours in the snow in zero degree weather, and for what, just a damn picture. Yes, it would have been beautiful. But the security I felt in your arms that day was beauty enough for me. I never felt scared in our arms, and I always felt alive. Where are you, baby? I need you now more than ever. I could use some of your light right now.

Shit, what, who the BANG! Damn, where did that thing come from? Why didn't I see it? Damn it; used another bullet. It worked, though; he fell just like the others. Their heads shoot them in the fucking head. I so wish I had more ammunition or maybe even an automatic rifle. What I wouldn't do for a machine gun right now. Gun shops, where is the closest gun store? That's right, no service. Those bastards took down all the cell towers in the area to cut us off from the rest of society. Maybe I can find a phone book when I find shelter, and I have to find some shelter soon. I feel those beasts closing in.

V

Those two must be close, and ironically, they seem to sense each other. I am sure that it won't be long until they finally meet again. I wonder who will survive that encounter? My money is on the shotgun, that chick seems to know exactly what she is doing. I just hope that she has enough ammo to keep her safe.

It's hard to believe that I am still moving forward tonight. Usually, by this time, both my medication has kicked in, and I am about to pass out. Or the accounts I am documenting have taken such an emotional toll on me that the voices and screams become real. Maybe this new stuff from the clinic is working, and it is finally allowing me to operate in a normal capacity. That would be such a nice change; it has been some time since I have been able to function in a normal capacity. It has been since I left Kuwait all those years ago. But, that was another time and place. Not to mention so much has happened to me in those years.

To finish up for the night, I figured it was time to check in with our damsel who is making her way into the house. Now, if I could only find her journal. Where is it? I can't believe that I have misplaced it. Honestly, it is one of my favorites. There it is. Now, where did we leave off?

February 14 (continued),

Hello, anyone there? That's what I said when I got inside. Look, baby, the house at last. I called again, hello... But, no one answered. It is so quiet and peaceful in here honey and best of all; we appear to be alone. We should be safe; I haven't seen any of those monsters in what seems like hours.

As I walked around the outside, I continued to call: hello... No one answered. It took me a while to climb those damn stairs out front, as I hoped that the house was unlocked. Everything looked to be in place, and the doors, windows, everything looked the same as I remembered it. Plus, luckily, I knew that there was an extra key hidden by the window under the small evergreen tree on the porch. From the look of it, I don't think any of those beasts have been here.

We should be safe now that we made it inside. Hold on baby, momma knows. I can feel your restlessness from all of the walking. We both need a rest. I promise, as soon as I finish this passage, I will sing you that lullaby, or one of those nursery rhymes that you love so much. I can feel you kick every time I go into one of them.

Luckily, we are alone baby, no one answered. I didn't even see signs of life as I walked the first floor. We have the whole house to ourselves. Once I find the tv, I will get to that nursery rhyme. I know you don't understand, but maybe the television or even the radio will have an idea of what is taking place out there. I know you are too young to comprehend, and you don't even know what I am writing about, but someday you will. It will only be a second honey; I found it. Oh my God, oh God, baby! Noooo! This can't be. I am going to write the message from the screen, so you know what we are up against.

"... This is a special bulletin from the emergency broadcast agency. All citizens of western Pennsylvania are encouraged to stay inside. Large unexplained outbreaks of bloodthirsty terrorists are on the loose. These vile predators are feasting on the flesh of every human walking. The governor has declared a state of emergency throughout

parts of the Keystone State. Neither the CDC nor NSA has a comment on the strange attacks.

All people are encouraged to stay within the confines of their homes or head directly to shelter. These creatures are extremely dangerous and appear invulnerable... "

CHAPTER FOURTEEN

"WHAT ARE THESE WHICH ARE ARRAYED IN WHITE ROBES?"

OCTOBER 29

Shut up! Please, just give me some damn quiet in here. I can't take much more. These cries, these screams, are killing me! Give me some love, some laughter, anything but these cries. I'm sorry, I know I shouldn't let these personal demons interfere with this project, but I can't help mentioning it. Everywhere I go, no matter what I do the screams and cries follow.

Nothing could be worse than yesterday at the clinic. I swear these screams were deafening. Maybe it's the season; maybe I have developed a hypersensitivity to the ghastly abominations on display throughout the town. This has to be the worst time of the year. Everyone is in a frenzy, and it seems even more than in years past, everyone is somewhat on edge this year. Maybe I should just barricade myself in here; it is quieter than outside. Shut the fuck up! Please, I beg you, stop it. No, my pills, I have to grab some pills.

All right, but before I do that and find something
to sooth, these unwanted voices, let me dive
back into what is important: the search for lovely
Gabrielle. Will her lover find her? Can she save him?
I can't wait to see where we are!

I

*(Click) I am lost. Where are you my beauty? I
can't seem to feel you anymore. Did you survive?
My mind is clouded, what is happening to me?
Everywhere I look, I see your eyes, those stunning
eyes staring back at me. Pale, vibrant, enduring,
they peer into my soul like nothing else. Are you
still there waiting for me? At the crossroad, which
way do I go? How can I find you? I have to; I will
never be the same if I can't hold you again. I lost
you once, and the depths of that misery left an
everlasting void inside my heart.*

*What's that smell? It's not you, my dear, but
from somewhere the pungent aroma of bliss
saturates this frozen expanse; it has to be the
splendor of a moist fount of redemption. Someone
is near, why can't it be you darling? Why do I
have to wait for your embrace? Am I truly that
hideous now; is it my eyes-my hands? Don't fear,
I promise when we meet again, the ecstasy will
overtake your pain, and the anguish will satisfy
every nerve in your body.*

*There it is again, where are you? Maybe you are
behind that door, or in that building? I know someone
is here. Anger, I can sense anger. I know you want
to kill me, but I can't help what I've become; I can't
stop these cravings. Please, don't punish me; there is
nothing I can do. Punish those bastards that made me
this way. I don't know if you can hear me, but I know*

you are here. I can feel you watching me. Now, I will have to find you. **(Click)**

II

Sorry about that last outburst, I am trying my best to push through. You know, I am honestly amazed that I have maintained motivation through the constant barrage of darkness. Yes, I did survive this outbreak and did have first-hand knowledge of what transpired, but I in no way endured the despair experienced by those who I am documenting. For me, it was like a flashback, or dream, from when I was in Bagdad, watching the innocent civilians fall to the repressive globalists' agenda.

That in itself is something you will never hear the truth about. Chelsea Manning attempted to bring this to light via WikiLeaks but quietly fell victim to the authoritarian government machine, set on persecuting whistleblowers instead of embracing them. In fact, the entire narrative of Operation Desert Storm was a lie. It was not about weapons of mass destruction, not about oil, not even about the invasion of Kuwait as many in the media speculated; plain and simple, it was about control. Look it up; the documents reveal that Saddam Hussein started to stand up to the United Nations establishment about the longstanding sanctions against his nation. For that act of disobedience, the United Nations/New World Order reigned down sentencing the Iraqi people with decades of strife. Ask yourself, who is the real enemy.

If you dig deeper into the anti-establishment nations or specifically Agenda 21/Agenda 2030, you will find a trend that will lead you back to the United Nations and their puppet masters: the Rothschild family. There you will find a small fact that those in the mainstream media or the government don't want you to know, the Middle Eastern nations that have fallen victim to oppression and a rise of Islamic terrorism at one time early in the century all lacked one thing: a Rothschild bank.

With these nations holding out, the United Nations could not completely manipulate the currency and global economy; therefore, their plan for world domination had to be put in abeyance. Why do I mention this? Easy, I want you to know about the ones responsible for this ghastly outbreak. It was our government, in the name of the United Nations, which led the charge for regime change in all these nations. Look at it for yourself, Iraq, Egypt, Libya, Syria, what do they look like today?

Looking back today, it is easy to see how weak over the last eight years. He was truly a puppet for these demonic bastards, and he sold out our freedom. Don't believe me? Look at how his decisions left a negative impact on society, not only here in America but across the globe. The highways of America are ravaged, Europe is in shambles, and people are suffering. Believe me yet? If not, look at how he created and armed ISIS and funded the rise of radical Islam. Lie after lie, yet the sheep continue to believe it, even though it has long been proven to be a reality.

This is another one of the myriads of reasons that I must push forth with thee accounts. Because many of these happenings were isolated to our little piece of Pennsylvania, countless Americans and a majority of the world's populace have no idea what transpired? They must see and hear what we endured at the hands of these beasts and the collective of degenerates that shroud themselves under that blue and white flag of injustice.

Speaking of crime, I believe that our lowly scientists have finally found shelter outside of the city. Of all of our players, these bastards deserve no sanctuary; I think they should have already passed on. They should have suffered the same fate of the others in the face of this plague. To me, their only chance at redemption will come if they discover a cure for this disease and find a way to save humanity.

III

(Play) Look, Mark, there it is. I knew we would make it out of that damn tunnel. Quick, over there, head into that cemetery before another one of those creatures sense our presence. I know we can find a tomb or crypt in there that we can use as a shelter, to get some rest. At this point, it appears that we escaped the confines of the city undetected. Most importantly, we made it unharmed, with hope to find some cure for this misery. But we both need a breather before that can happen, we must get some sleep.

I can't believe we are the only survivors. There had to be others that made out alive, that made it this far from the city. John put up a fight, but we both witnessed what can happen if you aren't prepared. All he had to do was listen to us, and I know he could be standing here with us tonight. I just hope that he wasn't forced to join them, and now he too is hunting us down.

There, in there, finally, an open crypt. Hurry, get inside, and help me bar the door. Mark, this may sound insane, but this may be the safest place for us right now. The lingering smell of decay that saturates the night sky should mask our scent; it should keep us safe (at least for the evening). Although, I can't be sure since I have no clue how these creatures think, or what caused the outbreak. Trust me; I wish I knew what caused this epidemic; everything would be easier as we move forward.

That's it, that steel door should keep us safe inside here. I just hope that the elders trapped in this tomb don't decide to stir. From what I have seen, that shouldn't be a problem; the disease does not appear to be airborne. Don't look at me like that. I know that is what I said about Ebola a few years ago, but this time I am positive that I am right. Plus, none of these bodies in here except us can breathe.

I still can't comprehend what went wrong. All I know is that there has to be a trigger. I just hope as I dissect my notes I can find something to help us break this genetic code and find a cure. Mark, go ahead, and take the first nap, I will watch over you. Trust me; nothing will happen to you! **(Stop)**

IV

I almost feel sorry for that man; the cross he carries must feel unbearable, the weight of humanity, the realization of creating a monster, a horde of monsters. At least Jesus bore his cross to save all human civilizations, not destroy it. Hearing him, I am sure his sins run deep. CIA, DARPA, WHO, UN, all torch bearers for the globalist hierarchy out to destroy us all. Fuck the UN; I never pledged my allegiance to that faggot white and blue flag. How dare they infect our shores with their genetic mutations?

You know, it's been that bastard Scotereo s' fault. Yes, Crentin and Prescott were sick and weak pledges in the international fraternity, but at least they did not apologize for our actions. Dare I say they loved America, something that for all intensive purposes can't be said about Scotereo? He was nothing more than a whipping boy for the globalists; a man more concerned with his image and his legacy than the country. He caved to the UN at every turn. You solely can't blame him, though. Dorner, Ayerson, Wrightman, Davids, fucking communist propagandists that radicalized him against America and the media and liberal snowflakes anointed him their savior.

We were doomed from the start, as this brainwashed fucking community organizer set out to destroy our nation with his spineless actions and apologetic agenda. Fuck, he created fucking ISIS in the name of oil and allowed their hijacked interpretation of Islam to rise and spread across the societies, to those bastards I say bring it. I will stand steadfast against you and impale you upon the upside-down cross you worship. You will never take our lands or change our beliefs; your caliphate will die here.

Although things have not improved significantly during this run up to the election, at least there is a chance that we can dodge that criminal globalist Heather Crentin, her rapist husband, and her spirit cooking administration. No matter how unhinged Alexander appears to be, it has to be better than four more years of Scotereos' treasonous policies. There is absolutely no way we could survive the open hemisphere ideology of the extreme left. I ask you, what is wrong with valuing Americans more that immigrants that want to change our society? My ancestors were immigrants, but unlike those of today, they loved the idea of a new culture inside the melting pot. Fortunately, they decided to adhere to the laws and raised their children to love the country.

Shut up! Please, shut up! Pills, I must find my pills. Those voices, and those screams, I can't take much more. Every time I raise my pen to scratch off something in my notes, I hear them. Why am I being tortured? I tried to save her; I tried to help them all. At the clinic they talk about Heaven, I will never see you in fucking heaven. I am a sinner; I am destined to spend eternity suffering in the depths of the pit. I wonder is that what the preacher was talking about when we left him? Could this child be the one; could this child our savior?

V

From the depths came flashes of lightning,
geysers of blood,
And cries of unfathomable anguish;
For the exiled beasts have risen before
the throne and the undead walk.
Seven Fallen Souls, seven evils to plague man-
Through the head and blood, a lost light will shine,
And the light will be known as redemption.

(*The Revelation of Moloch* 8.12)

Father, again I stand before you and call to thee. My faith is strong, but still my resolve wavers. I can sense the chosen one secluded inside the corridors of this sanctuary, yet I cannot find him. Where is he? Why am I failing you? Our congregation continues to grow with every step; still, I feel we are falling short of your expectations. Are our prayers not loud enough?

Father, did you receive our last offering? Could you not taste the sweetness in her loins? Her tears

were in harmony with the holiest of waterfalls,
and her pleas for absolution were legendary even
in this Hell. Father, was I not right to sacrifice
her? Did I betray your trust? I was sure you would
enjoy her flesh and accept her into your world.
Her pain was justified; she was a blasphemer.

As I stand upon this mount, I again beg you for
a sign. Please, give all of us the strength to remain
vigilant during our journey. Father, please give
us the guidance we need to fulfill our true destiny
here on Earth. Let us seed the next generation
of followers, baptize them in the sacred fire, and
enlighten the world with your glory.
Let us pray.

Lord of Light
Out might is strong through your words
Yet, our souls weep from the emptiness
Guide us through our Midbar and Chorbah
And all of the fruits ripened on the vines
For our power grows inside each of us
Our souls cowering to your majesty
Enlightened by the signs left before us
Another sacrifice nears, your sacred grail ahead
In your name, we pray
Amen

VI

Prayers, I think we all need some prayers in our
lives. I am not saying that we all need religion or
a zealot masquerading as the antichrist leading
us through mass, but prayer is real. Hell, I don't
personally care who you pray to; God, Allah,
Jehovah, Xemu, Buddha, Satan, Yourself, just pray.
Who knows, maybe through prayer these fucking

voices will go away, trust me, I know you can hear them too.

What's that, gunshots? I hate Halloween, and I can tell it is almost upon us. The patrols are picking up outside. I guess the militarized police force want to try out those new armored vehicles. Shut up! Please, I beg-no I pray, that you will just shut the fuck up. Can't you see I am trying to concentrate here? I want to continue. Oh God, not again! The screams, the laughter, make it stop; make it all stop! Please God, anyone, help me!

CHAPTER FIFTEEN

"...AND GOD SHALL WIPE AWAY ALL TEARS FROM THEIR EYES."

OCTOBER 30

Hello again, I figured that I would settle in and get some more work done tonight, although I am not sure how long I can spend sitting here at my computer. Tomorrow is Halloween, and the noise outside is becoming deafening. I swear someone is watching me. No shit, with every breath I take or with every step, I can feel the eyes stare through me.

Of course, the people at the clinic tell me it's just my imagination playing tricks on me; that these are just some of the side effects from the medication. But, I know they are mistaken. Someone or something is watching my every move. Hell, even now I can sense that there is something in this room with me as I sit at the computer. I'm not fucking around; something is here; the screams, the laughter, the giggles, strange noises that continue to pierce the quiet inside my apartment. Why can't these nightmares just go away? I am awake; I have to be awake.

All right, let me refocus. I have to get back into the journey I am leading you through. I do wonder if you will find these accounts as necessary as I do. I hope so. These accounts are our history; the truth of what happened when the globalists' evil plan backfired. The world deserves, no, must understand exactly what we went through and the depths that these reptilian elites will go to achieve their goals.

I know what you are thinking, enough already. I guess I have been rambling a bit more than usual tonight and I know that's not why you are here. You want to hear from our heroine, Gabrielle. How is she; is she safe secluded in the house by herself? Is she alone? Like you, I hope she is. I couldn't imagine continuing with this project if she was gone. If anyone needs to survive throughout this ordeal, it is she.

I

February 15, 2014,

Wow, baby that kick! I know you are scared, but I am here to protect you. I think I have us secured down here in the basement. I am finally able to relax, and I promise after I finish this entry, I will get to that story I promised. At this point, I have no idea what to say to you. Could you hear that message on the television? I know you can hear music when I play it for you, I can feel you move inside of me. I'm not going to lie to you; I want you to know when you are old enough to read this that I am scared. I don't know what more I can do or how much more I can take. These monsters are everywhere; they are probably surrounding us right now.

I just want to know where you father is. He never seems to be around when I need him. I wish he were here with us, I always feel safe in his arms. He is a great man and I know he would protect us from these beasts if he were with us right now. Are you tired? You seem to be settling down. I am almost done, and then we can take a power nap after your story.

Thank God, we were able to find this house. Old farmhouses are the perfect places to hide when things go awry. There are always many surprises to be found, and more importantly, they are littered throughout this region. This is just a small bit of advice for you when you read this in a few years. Of course, I would rather share this information with you myself, but I can't guarantee that I will survive this nightmare. If I don't, you will always have this journal to look back upon and know what happened to us. Let's hope that is not the case.

Hold on baby; I have to get up and check behind that door. I heard something over there. I believe it is the old coal chute and either something is in there, or something is trying to get in. Personally, I pray it is nothing but my imagination. I can't believe I overlooked that door. That is the only room I didn't check before I barricaded the door. I'm sure it's nothing. That story is coming, I promise.

II

Coal chutes, I thought those were all phased out over the past few decades. Once the war on coal began under old man Prescott and then Crentin with his climate change wacko Moore by his side, it seemed inevitable that these entryways would be removed in the name of energy efficiency. This is just another reason why these retarded climate change agendas should be outlawed. Fucking United Nations, climate change my ass, cycles-the fucking Earth orbits in different cycles of proximity to the sun.

You know, it pisses me off just thinking about that crap. Climate change is just another excuse for the globalists to control society their retarded carbon tax plan to bleed people dry in the name of fear. Well, guess what? Al Gore's doomsday clock has expired, and we are still here, the ice caps are still here, and California did not sink into the Pacific (although, some wish it would have). Damn government, you bastards again should worry more about Americans instead of hijacking our sovereignty to grease the palms of your technocrat puppet master's

Fuck you Prescott and your New World Order bullshit, you too Crentin and Scotereo. Your weakness and hatred of America is something we will never forget. How could you bow down before the United Nations and sell out our population? Our founding fathers have to be rolling in their graves by your lack of respect for our Constitution. I for one hope you all rot in Hell.

...Sorry, sorry, I didn't mean to go off on another one of my unnecessary tangents. There are just times where I can't help but vent. It's just that none of the atrocities I have written about ever needed to happen. Had one of these bastards been a patriot, we wouldn't be here today. Instead, it is just another example of the lies being told by the elite of our nation, just like the battle with ISIS (or ISIL); our government has betrayed us and is responsible for the entire fiasco.

Oh well, enough of that, time to get back to our journey. Where were we? I know it has been some time since we've checked in on Morgan. The more

I break down her story; I get the feeling that there is more going on with her than I initially imagined. Something just doesn't feel right with her accounts, its almost like she is hiding something, and this secret weighs heavily on her.

I still can't believe you are gone, Esther. Damn it, why couldn't I protect you? I made a promise, no, I swore to you that I would be there when you needed me. I just wasn't strong enough. Now, I'm the one that needs you; now I'm the one that is in trouble. I feel walled in. I am surrounded by these beasts and have no clue where to go. Plus, I am running low on ammo, and I have no idea where I can find some more. I think there is a plaza ahead with a gun shop. I just can't be sure. Too much has happened to me in these last few hours that I just can't process anything. I just know that I need to find some ammo.

A drug store would be nice as well. Esther, you have my medication, and I can feel, it starting to wear off. I knew the doctor should have upped my dosage. Looking around, this may not be the best time, considering the situation with the amount of adrenaline I am using. I hate how I feel when this happens. What am I going to do? You know that I can't go back.

Look, up there, it's a small group of those creatures. Fuck, only two shells, there is nothing I can do with only two shells. I wonder is there anything else I can use. There is nothing around me. I will have to find a place to hide; maybe I can break into one of these buildings to buy some time. I don't think I have any other choice but to find some shelter and let the streets clear. This place should work. And it's unlocked.

III

Now what, fuck, is that thunder? Fuck, it is, thunder! Why can't I just have one fucking night of silence? It wasn't supposed to storm tonight. Why is everything so loud? The screams, the thunder, the voices, everything just echoes inside my mind. It's a jumbled mess feeding the turmoil; I swear it just fuels my hatred for these disgusting degencrates. Fuck all of you, why must you torment me?

I'm not sure how much more I can get through tonight. Between the sudden flashes, the thunder, and the voices, I just want to lock myself up and be done with life for a night. I really can't take much more of this torture and I know tomorrow will be worse. Halloween has become such a nightmare in the city. The children knocking on doors, the myriad of patrols, and the emotions, I wish they would outlaw it. There has to be another alternative to trick-or-treating and costumes. I mean, didn't they get enough of that shit when our town were infested by the vile plague? I know I did.

With it being Halloween tomorrow, I know that I have to push through some more of this, though, at least one more account. After this, I have no clue when I will be back at the computer. So, one more before I lock myself up for the evening (and highly medicate myself), shut up! Please, no more voices, I beg of you, no more. Oh well, I guess I will make this a short one with our host. I wonder what type of emotions he felt as he struggled through his mutation (man to plague); I wonder if he was able to process the true depths of depravity. Personally, I couldn't even start to imagine the emotional toll he went through during this ordeal.

IV

(Click) The blood and bile of the meek surround me. I am trapped in this nightmare and I can't wake up. I am so afraid to take another step. This craving, this hunger is overwhelming me. With every step I take, my mind is consumed by the thought of the deliciousness sealed by your loins. Everywhere I look, I can hear the faint heartbeats of life around me: salvation grows.

Gabrielle, what have I become? Around every corner, I can smell the freshness of life and want to experience it. A sanguine stream leads me to the pleasures of the flesh, and I dine, no, feast upon the innocents, their essence fulfills all desires. Every bite washed down with the blessed blood of thy Father. I swear; they taste so sweet upon my dying tongue.

No, Gabrielle, am I not already dead to you? I have to be. I know I died the day we said goodbye and shared one final embrace overlooking the fountain. I wish it were different; I wish that it never happened. I remember it so clearly. Your pale skin, flushed breasts, your pale blue eyes stared deep into mine with words left unspoken. Now, they are destined to span a lifetime of loneliness; just like me if I can't find you. I know it's my fault. Why was I so wrong? Why did I say goodbye? You were my world and I never wanted to lose you.

I know you are out there. I can feel your warmth somewhere close to me. Are you out there watching over me? Are you the beauty I have been following? I pray that you are, and for the day, I can prey on your flesh and finally consummate our love for all eternity. I love you. (Click)

CHAPTER SIXTEEN

"AND THERE APPEARED ANOTHER WONDER IN HEAVEN, AND BEHOLD A GREAT RED DRAGON..."

OCTOBER 31

Go away; I don't have any fucking candy! Fuck! It's only two fucking o'clock in the afternoon, why aren't these demonic hooligans in school? I couldn't make it to the clinic, let alone back home, without being besieged by these ungracious vultures begging for fucking candy. I don't get it, when I was a kid; we at least followed the prescribed rules. We may not have liked them or agreed with them, but we had respect for people and their policies. Not today, these little degenerates have little to no regard for anything or anyone. I guess that's what happens when everyone gets a trophy.

I can't take much more of this and it is still early in the day. I honestly hate Halloween and the suffering it ushers in. I see reminders of the atrocities that I witnessed and endured everywhere I look. I can't take the rush of emotions and the fears that overtake my already fractured sanity. Why did I have to survive and be forced to live with this curse? I swear, it is a punishment worse than death; these voices and visions drive me deeper into the pit of despair every day and I am ready to meet my maker.

Who knows, maybe the doctors at the clinic and my friend(s) are right. Perhaps I should give up this project and stop my quest to document the evils that I observed. Honestly, what is it accomplishing? Anger, pain, misery, is this torture worth it? Give in to my affliction, which is what everyone wants me to do. But, it's not quite that easy, and I'm not sure that the visions or voices will go away if I did. The silence often makes it worse and even if they don't understand it, these words often help me push through the day. They help me survive and give me hope inside this miserable society we call home.

It's funny; I once had faith in humanity, but now I have nothing. I am surrounded by emptiness, loneliness, and sorrow; those fucking bastards took everything I ever loved or cared for. Fuck them! Fuck all of them! Talk about faith, I know one man on this journey that demonstrated unwavering faith. Through this whole nightmare, he gave his followers a foundation to lean upon as turmoil erupted everywhere. Sure, we can argue if he was on the right side of the battle that was taking place around us, but that is a discussion better left for another day.

I

While the son watched the mighty sun
fall behind the mount,
A voice whispered inside him and
a vision replaced the sky,

For a brother was near,
And his salvation was closer.

(The Revelation of Moloch 9.10)

Behold, the sinners are growing by the thousands. Can you smell them and their unholy shroud of sin? Their tainted scent saturates the night sky. From here, I can taste their fear, their unsanctified souls calling for forgiveness. Listen close, hear their confessions, and make them bow before thy Father and receive the penitence they deserve.

Beware the false prophets that walk among them. For the prophesized one remains within their grasp. We must continue to be steadfast in our search for his light and stand strong in the face of his supreme powers. The followers of the false prophets will try to protect him, even though the know naught about his divine message. Thy Father has forewarned us of their deceit and the dangers we will face in our battle to save humanity.

Our salvation is tied to their defeat. We must reach out and find the infected and help them find their way to the cross. They must suffer the pain of the spikes and feel the flames of righteousness overtake their flesh. Their suffering must be legendary in both Heaven and Hell. Let it be known across all worlds that neither child nor man shall try to rise above the almighty.

Through our vigilance, we will protect our fields and our flock from these false prophets, and open the gate of redemption before the pit. As our congregation grows, the Scriptures become clear. We must stand at the prefaces of freedom, and there, at last, we can right the millennia of torture Thy Father has endured at the hand of the immoral

Trinity. We will, at last, be the torchbearers of light and our destiny will be fulfilled.
Let us pray.

Lord of Light
Upon this field, our hearts beat in unison
For, through your wisdom, everything is again clear
Our path has been foretold, and we grow stronger with ever bite
Now, quench our thirst for knowledge,
And allow your light to guide us through desolation
Accept our sacrifice and hear our prayers,
For our strength is fulfilled by your divinity
And our destiny is fulfilled by your prudence
In your name, we pray
Amen

II

Shut up! My head is pounding. I can't believe how bad these headaches have become. Plus, with these damn kids, their costumes, and the delight they take at watching my misery increase with every rap upon the door. At one time, I used to love this time of the year, this season. Honestly, who wouldn't? Between the cooler temperatures, the legends, and the lore, it was incredible. I remember spending hours reading about the Salem Witch Trials, the occult, and the local supernatural folklore, but not now. Those are just memories of a life long forgotten.

I have not forgotten about you baby. I never would forget what we had. You are my hero, and the one giving me the courage to push forward with this manuscript. Have you forgiven me yet? Would you return to share my bed, to make love to me? What, shut up, what am I saying? I failed you; I watched them take you, and I watched them consume your flesh. Your entrails were likely spread everywhere. I am still disturbed by the thought, I can almost see them standing over you like a sacrifice upon an altar. They are violating you in unfathomable ways; I can almost hear the crunch of your fragile bones as their teeth defiled your beauty and within these visions feel the pain of the claws tearing through your womb.

Just the thought of you still haunts me. The voices and whispers are driving me to the edge of sanity. I can't take much more of the solitude or dreams. They are destroying me. Everywhere I look, I see remnants of you, and I feel your anguish and hear your screams. Every time I close my eyes, I see the crimson streams of tears flowing from your lifeless skull. Know what, you were still smiling; through the agony, the smile never left your face.

I just wonder, are you in Heaven? Did God shine down upon you and grant you a seat in paradise? I wish we could meet again, and I could see your beauty one more time. Unfortunately, that can never happen, for I'm not worthy of eternal glory. I'm a monster; I let you die and did nothing to help you. I am a coward. Shut Up! Please, shut up! These screams must stop! This project, I must force myself to work on it. I have to finish before it kills me. Our scientists, where were they?

III

(Play) This vile disease, what have I done? How could I have created such a mutation? What have I become? It seems like only yesterday all my work was for the good of man. I wanted to save humanity from the devastating plagues that have ravaged our world. I wanted to eradicate all disease and save the planet. I wanted to save lives, not start the apocalypse.

Damn you Bethesda, why did I let you corrupt me? I thought we were saving people, not destroying them. They were so young; pure, and we took advantage of their helplessness. We became monsters. Our experiments, the suffering, the brainwashing, it sullied them. Their losses, their torment, all left debilitating scars hidden deep within them. Yes, we cannot see them, but they are there creating a single torture chamber in their minds. And we are responsible. Is this my punishment?

I cannot believe how those days early in my internship changed me. I embraced the depravity; I became a monster. First, it was the dark ops I was recruited for in rogue CIA labs such as Dulce, Montauk, and Homan Square and programs such as Ultra, Search, and Naomi. We started with their minds, and to an extent, their souls. We couldn't stay there, though; we had to play God. Now, it's much worse; we started experimenting on their bodies.

Indeed, I have become a monster. I am just like those rancid beasts outside. I should be out there with them; I should be a mindless vassal craving the flesh of man, tracking everyone in search for my next meal. That's why we're here trapped inside this decaying chamber. That is why we will likely die in here. My notes, yes, my notes; the secret to what is happening must be there. Was it one of the drugs, or trial vaccines? I wouldn't think so; there was no sign of any crazy side effects in the rats. They were all healthy, weren't they? Was I blinded by the potential accolades and overlooked something?

My journals, the answers have to be in my journals. I have to wonder, though, are we the only ones suffering through this strange uprising? Is this happening at other facilities? If that's the case, this may not be my fault. Maybe I am blaming myself for nothing. Yes, that's it. No, can't get excited, I know the truth. It was I; it has always been me. I am a monster. **(Stop)**

IV

Stop, I have to stop it tonight. As much as I want to continue, especially with the revelation that Doctor Mengele is finally reaching the conclusion that many of us have already achieved; he's a piece of shit! Figures, just when reality starts to set in with one of the people I am documenting, these damn voices return. Why, why did these voices have to come back? Why Lord, can you tell me that? If you are truly the almighty, all-knowing creator, why have you cursed me into damnation?

I have tried to understand, but I just can't do it. I can't go on much longer. My head feels as if it's about to explode. I have no choice but to take these godforsaken pills and lock myself in my room. I just have to make these screams go away. I know I should have done that earlier; in fact, I should have just secluded myself all day. That way those damn kids outside wouldn't be harassing me. I swear those heathens outside are far worse than the creatures I am documenting on these pages.

Fuck, I am so sorry about this, I didn't mean to have another set of entries cut short because of my afflictions. Go away already! I want to keep rolling; I want to finish this manuscript so the truth can be known. It doesn't look like that will happen, though. Maybe later once everything calms down, I'll be able to return to sanity and finish this entry. God, I hope I can, I have to know what he finds.

I may also have to make a trip into the dark web though before I jump back into stuff. I want to look up some of these programs. I have heard about MK Ultra, but what it Search and Naomi? And, what is the Bethesda he mentions? I know it is a Naval hospital and medical center; I have been there a few times. I just can't imagine there being a Deep State, black ops lab there; especially when he mentions Dulce and Montauk in a separate thought. I guess it could be underground like Montauk, but still, that just feels like a stretch.

Shut up already! These damn kids are killing me tonight. Why aren't you done with the fucking candy already? Isn't Halloween over? Leave me alone, please, I can't take it anymore. Go away! Stop calling me, stop the knocking, and just leave me alone. Please, just let this dreadful night come to an end.

CHAPTER SEVENTEEN

"...AND UPON HIS HEADS
THE NAME OF BLASPHEMY."

NOVEMBER 4

I know I haven't written anything for a few days, but I haven't had the energy to get back to the computer. I changed medication, and the adjustment period has made me quite lethargic. Couple that with the dismal weather, and I just have not had the motivation to do anything. The weather has been so gray and dreary, I can't believe the amount of rain that has come down, and you would think we were stuck in a hurricane. I had better be quiet, if Al Gore heard me say that, he would be here pushing for more carbon taxes and want to limit my electricity.

I will apologize now; I also hadn't done much research on the operations mentioned by our scientist before I had to stop the other night. I couldn't find the energy for that either. I did make it to the clinic for a group session before having my medication changed. It was strange; I swear I saw one of those militarized convoys through the mist as I was walking over there.

I know that's impossible, those have been gone for a few years. Plus, I doubt they would be brazen enough to try to sneak into the city with their pawn Scotereo leaving office. This could be a different time and place, one where the laws of the land are enforced.

Incredibly, that was the last hallucination type of event to hit me. With this new experimental drug, all of the visions and voices have disappeared. Other than the sluggishness, I feel like a new man. Maybe this combination of medications and therapy are finally starting to work. I guess only time will tell, right?

All is not perfect, though, the emptiness I feel inside is there, and I still have a void in my heart that nothing has been able to fill. When I lost you, I lost a part of myself. I lost who I was and who I was going to be. I honestly never realized how much you meant to me until it was too late. Now, I am stuck with just memories and pictures, all of my hopes and dreams are gone.

Speaking of being too late, our scientist seemed to be waking to some harsh facts. For the first time, I believe he realizes that the agencies he served are not what they seem. They are not out for the good of mankind; they are evil. They are searching for world domination and population control. If only he would have realized this earlier, we may not be here right now. Although, as compartmentalized as these organizations are and with the multifaceted web of shadow activities also involved with these operations, that was likely impossible.

I

(Play) What have I missed? As I go through this data, none of the drugs that were used should have ever created such a deadly contagion. The cause of this outbreak seems to sit outside the bounds of my work. I have looked deep into my notes, the combination of Xanoxopan and Detrohydrozine have been through a rigorous set of independent tests and both animal and human trials over the past decade, and no side effects such as this have ever been recorded. Hell, even the rats did not go crazy.

According to this data, the worst side effect was an occasional case of hemorrhaging, especially from the eyes, but those were isolated to test subjects that showed signs of an iron deficiency. There was nothing like this, though. What is different now? What is the alien antibody that is causing such a devastating side effect on everyone that has come in contact with this experiment?

Mark, do you happen to have the results of the last blood test after you ran them through the mass spectrometer? I can't remember if I ever broke those numbers down and entered them into the medical records. That data could show us something we may have overlooked. Thanks; let me see what we have. 30 percent Xanoxopan, 40 percent Detrohydrozine, 8 percent Barium, 15 percent Aluminum, and 7 percent Thorium? What the hell, where did that combination come from? Aluminum, Barium, and Thorium, I have never seen that combination of chemicals in a lab setting (especially mine). There was a rumor that a Dr. Tsarnovski was experimenting with it as a way of cooling the atmosphere, but that was back in the early1990s.

Fucking bastards, I never took those damn chemtrails outside into account when working out my hypothesis. The air we breathe could impact how our bodies react to certain substances, especially the chemtrail cocktails that are being developed. I have heard whispers that the super flu is being developed that can be triggered by the chemical compounds released into the atmosphere. I honestly thought it was a joke; no one would want to do that, would they? I swear, if this is what caused this outbreak, I will get even with everyone involved and expose them for the world to see.

Mark, I bet this is where the contamination entered into our equation. Now, we need to prove this theory, somehow, we need to test the air outside, especially if they are spraying. We need t find a lab, or a house, and capture one of those creatures. We need their blood to compare against our records and the air samples. If we can verify our findings, we should be able to find (or develop) a cure. **(Stop)**

II

Fucking chemtrails! I knew they were more than just exhaust residue streams from the new jetliners. I have been saying that forever, and being called crazy the whole time. No one ever wants to hear the truth. My evidence was obvious and simple, why didn't I see these trails when I was a kid? When was the technology not as advanced? The answer is simple because they didn't exist. It wasn't until that fucker George Prescott was in office that they started popping up across the sky. Next thing you know, that bastard Gore started talking about extinction from global warming melting the ice caps. Coincidence? I don't believe coincidences exist.

Come to think of it, I haven't seen any of them in the skies over the past few years. I know the travel industry and the airlines have suffered quite a bit during this recession, but there are still planes in the sky every day and if this is just exhaust gas, why have the trails dissipated?

The further I get into this project, it becomes clear that the United Nations sits at the heart of the majority of problems that pop up throughout the world. Those fucking bastards! I have been telling you throughout this project that those globalist dictators should be held accountable, do you agree with me yet? Don't you think those pieces of shit should hang for their crimes against humanity? Public execution that would make a statement and maybe the elites would start to back off with their plans of world domination.

Hopefully, projects such as this one and some of the other outlets that are fighting the state-run narrative will start to have an impact. Maybe people across the globe will continue to wake up and be willing to expose the truth to the masses. It's time to face the reality that those fucking elite assholes want us dead. They want the planet for themselves in an exact manner that the Guidestones outline. To that, I say, fuck you!

Whew, sorry about the rambling, sometimes I can't control my emotions and that was one of them. That outburst did give me some added motivation to dive back into things. I think this would be a superb time to gain some calm and resolve. I believe that we should get back to our beautiful Gabrielle and her unborn son. I wonder what happened since we left off. If I remember right, she was facing some turmoil after she locked herself in the basement of that house.

III

February 15 (Continued),

Thank God baby, it was just a cat behind that
door. I guess that is the next best thing to my
imagination. I was so scared that it would be one
of those beasts, and honestly, I wasn't ready for
that. I am exhausted. Between all of the running
and emotional turmoil, I can't take much more
before I collapse. Plus, you have been battering
my insides lately. I know I swore you would never
play football, but you may have a future as a
kicker. You hear that right, not soccer, football.
Your father always said soccer was a girl's sport
and I agree with him.

Don't you worry, though; we will get some rest
soon. But, before we can do that and take our nap, I
owe you a story. As I was checking the door, I thought
of a perfect one for tonight. It may sound a little
different than the standard classics, but it is rooted
in the fabled world of Aesop. This one is called *The
Alien on the Farm,* and I wrote it a few years ago for a
college class when you were only a dream.

I know that you probably don't understand all
of this, but because of the strange situation we
are in, I think this story will fit the mood. After we
survive, when you are older and I finally allow you
to read this journal, ask me to see the copy of the
book I had made. I hoped (OK knew) that someday
I would have a child and I wanted to ensure that
they had some reading material that sat outside the
mainstream selections.

Now onto that story, then, finally, we can get some
well-deserved sleep. I love you...

IV

I can't believe how alive I feel on this new medication. In the past, by this point in the evening, the visions and voices would be overtaking my mind. There would be no way that I could be moving forward with anything, especially after the emotional account that I just finished. Plus, I am so alive, so coherent; everything is starting to make more sense and it has become easier to put pieces together.

Looking back at the last account, that children's book sounds interesting, aliens have always fascinated me. Ever since I heard the story about the Kecksburg UFO incident, I consumed everything I could find on the subject. I can't believe that we are the only being in the universe. Think about it, with the sheer size of the cosmos; it would be impossible to see no other form of life out there.

It's funny, though, there are many similarities between the Kecksburg incident and the account that I am documenting. Not only the general area (Kecksburg is about 40 miles from here) but with the massive build-up of military and government officials at the crash site and in town. Even with the eyewitness accounts, there is no certified government documentation or physical evidence to be found. Around every corner, researchers continually run into crazy roadblocks.

I'm quite familiar with all of this. Years ago, when I was researching Kecksburg for an article I was working on, I couldn't find one shred of legitimate evidence from the government. Plus, there were a few strange coincidences that took place, that seemed more sinister than real. After a talk with John Predistra (yes, the one from the emails), I submitted a Freedom of Information Act (FOIA) request for specific case files on Kecksburg. Within days of the submission, a military office threatened to revoke my security clearance. Message received loud and clear...

Over the years, I have continued my research on Kecksburg and just like was the case with my initial research for this project, the government has no documentation on anything that took place during this plague. Nothing, zip, zilch, according to them, nothing happened here. By this point, I am sure if you are reading this, you are convinced I am crazy and imagining all of this, that this entire work is fictional, but I swear that is not the case. All of this happened; I know it did.

Plus, I wasn't the only one that encountered the different governmental agencies; others faced the organized military apparatuses that were here on our shores. If I thinking straight, when I was sorting through the files, I believe one of our characters had a run-in with a group that appeared to be an international coalition of United Nations soldiers just outside of the tunnels. That is something that I hope would never happen under President Trump (if he is elected). Although, I don't think any of us know what to expect with him.

Now, where is that account and which character was it? Hold on; I believe it is our mysterious heroine who found her way into that unlocked building. In fact, I'm pretty sure that her observations of those foreign forces take place from inside that building. Now, where was it? Oh, yeah, here it is.

I think I am safe in here. Thank God, it was unlocked. I still wish I had my medication or some more shells. I looked through the downstairs rooms, nothing. No guns, no ammo; there is nothing that I could use as a weapon. Hopefully, daylight will arrive soon and I can make my way to one of those stores without running into trouble out there.

Damn it. I wish you were here with me. As I look out this window, I can't help but wonder what happened to you. Hey, what is that? It sounds like a Humvee, but I don't recognize the colors or markings. It does not look like something from our military, between the white color and the lack of identifying flags, maybe it is the police. If that's the case, it's about fucking time!

Maybe it is the police; over the past few years, President Scotereo has gone out of his way to militarize private law enforcement agencies across the country. Could this be some of those armored personnel carriers? I guess it could, but those uniforms I see through the windshield do seem familiar. I wish you were here to see this with me; you always were more up on the happenings and had a better memory of color schemes and fashion. That's why I always turned to you; I know nothing of those subjects.

Wow, there is another survivor in the building across the street. She is pounding on the window and waving the men in the Humvee down. Hopefully, they see her and maybe I can follow suit and be saved. They are stopping; they must see her. They are getting out and shining a spotlight in her direction. Funny, I still don't recognize the uniforms, though. White and blue colors, what agency wears those? That tall man seems to be in charge, and

*it looks like he is giving that gunner an order, I
wonder if they are going to send in a rescue team?*

*Wait, what, what the fuck are they doing? (Pop,
pop, pop, pop, pop) Fuck, they are shooting at her.
What the hell, I thought they were going to save
me. Quiet, I must stay silent. Fuck, what the Hell!*

V

White armored vehicles, white and blue uniforms;
that could only be the United Nations. All right,
the Soviets in the 1980s also had something
similar with their winter fatigues, but I am
pretty sure that they did away with those after
the end of the Cold War. Honestly, this is just
more proof that this was a synchronized globalist
attack organized by the United Nations. Although
some of the details have blurred through the
years, there are so many similarities between the
responses here on our shores and those put in
place during the Malaria outbreaks in Somalia and
the quarantine protocols used in Liberia during
their Ebola pandemic.

The bigger question is if it was the United
Nations, why were they here in the first place?
Think about it. They would have had to know this
was going to happen if they already had a military
contingent in place. Why else would the armored
vehicles be here? They must have been financing
the experiments and realized there was a chance
of a mutation and that is not right in my book.

Those bastards should not be on our shores,
experimenting on our citizens. I bet that is how
the rise of opioid abuse started; we all know that
the war in Afghanistan was really over the opium
and not terrorism. We have to get those bastards

out of our communities and they must be stopped. We must band together and send them back to one of the countries they already destroyed.

CHAPTER EIGHTEEN

"I AM HE THAT LIVETH, AND WAS DEAD; AND, BEHOLD, I AM ALIVE FOR EVERMORE..."

NOVEMBER 5

Hello again. I'm glad to be back with everyone this afternoon. I have to admit; I feel a buzz that I haven't felt in a long time. For the first time in what seems like forever, I am excited to continue with our journey. But, who wouldn't be excited, there is so much to talk about and so many histories to be told. Plus, on a positive note, this makes it almost a week without the visions and voices. It seems that once Halloween passed and all the signs of the militarized police forces disappeared from our streets, I started to feel alive again.

While things are moving toward a mass awakening, I still believe that we should have all seen through the veil of hypocrisy, and realized the underlying evil inside the New World Orders' ideology. All of the signs were there; I guess we just didn't want to know exactly how much the dark globalist state was in control of our every move or the depravity of their agenda.

Ironically, we were warned about this degeneracy many times in the past. Presidents such as Eisenhower, Kennedy, and even Reagan discussed these issues; hell, even John Lydon from the Sex Pistols warned of the background of Queen and her potential in human origins. At least now, some of us are awake and more people are waking every day.

I do have, to be honest with you today; I will stop the babbling. After we had wrapped things up, I went back in for some editing, and I realized how much I was rambling. I can assure you that won't happen today. In fact, I doubt I get more than one or two accounts in before I have to stop; I have a date tonight with that girl I met at the clinic. I know picking up a date at the hospital may sound strange, but she seems so different than many of the others and with any luck, we will keep our discussions off this topic.

I hope we can stay away from conversations about the blood and despair. She is usually rather quiet, but I know that if I can still see the pools of crimson and the body parts littered through the streets, she can as well. It was like a war zone; except, it was here on our soil. I can only imagine what it the streets looked like during our legendary apocalypse and the aftermath of the bones and bile at Antietam. Well, enough about that I think it is time to get rolling with our next account. I believe that it is time to visit our man of cloth; he is always so forthright and thought provoking.

I

*From deep within the darkness,
the Almighty spoke and the sun wept.
Open your soul to life and set forth*

across a new horizon,
For the signs of life rise,
And the prophesized one grows stronger.

(The Revelation of Moloch 9.12)

Look my children and behold the gospel as we move forward through damnation. As was foretold by the Wise Men of the West and sealed by the blood of our ancestors, unlike Mary, Joseph, and Richard, it is again Thy Father who has again perfected life. A true savior of humanity is again poised to walk among us. We must continue to push forth, to convert the unfaithful, and protect our redeemer from their sinful ways. As our numbers build, the prophecy of Our Father is at hand.

The sacred papyrus bleeds tears of truth and the sinners flee from their deeds. Their faith wavers as they prepare for the rapture. Come with me; help me tempt them with the purity of flesh. And, through that flesh, all of their sins will be forgiven. We must stand tall to complete our sacred passage. As Thy Father states in heavenly scripture, our journey to deliverance will be painful. But through that agony, our place in the Kingdom will be reserved for eternity.

Let us pray.

Lord of Light
I am humbled by the bestowed responsibility
Our hearts beat in unison with your Wisdom
And our minds are open to your guidance
We bow before you in awe, awaiting your blessing
Fill our souls with light and our bodies with strength
Lead us to the gates of temptation

And we shall justify your faith
In your name, we pray
Amen

II

Mary, Joseph, and Richard, who are they? What do they have to do with our dilemma, anything? I am going to have to step up my research. I know I have been slacking over the past few days. I don't think I have sat down at my computer to do anything except write. I know it is something that I have to do; I just can't seem to stay focused on the smaller details.

Damn it; look at the time and she's still not here. I was holding out hope that she would have been here by now. I guess she hasn't left work yet. Maybe I should call her. No, I don't want to seem impatient; I want everything to go smoothly tonight. You will have to forgive my excitement; it has been quite some time since I went on a date. Honestly, it's been a couple of years. It's been so long that I don't even remember how to act or what to do with a woman. I know, I know, just relax, and be myself. What could go wrong with that?

I just hope everything goes smoothly and the night isn't awkward. I do wonder if she will like me or if we will get along by ourselves. I will admit I think that things are a lot simpler in a group setting where the focus is spread between everyone involved in the session. I can only hope that same comfort carries over to our date when we are alone.

I guess it is the time that I get back to writing. It looks like I have a few more minutes before she arrives and this will help me pass my time. Where should I go? Which one of our characters will give me some pleasant thoughts before I depart? I think our lonely lover in search of Gabrielle would be fitting. I bet she is beautiful, at least I know he thinks so.

III

(Click) Beloved darkness, where shall I search from here? If only you could open your arms, embrace my remains, and guide me to my absent maiden. I am lost within this haunting maze and my mind is consumed by the thought of her beauty. This disease may have destroyed my flesh, but it is her, charming Gabrielle, that has stolen my soul.

As every second passes, I shamble through the night searching for that sparkle of an eye. Through the moonlight, I can taste her sanguine scent. My thoughts long for the delights felt in the gentle caress of our bodies near or the satisfaction held in the pulsating veins. Please, Gabrielle, I call to you. I long for you to entice me with the pleasures of your flesh and guide me through every inch of your being. Only together, can we illuminate the flame of hope and make this dream become a reality.

Gabrielle, can you hear me? Why are you so quiet? Do you not share the same thoughts and passions that I hold dear? Is there someone else out there sharing the warmth of your bed? Soon, the chilled gloom surrounding me will overtake sanity and the brisk winds that howl across the empty moonlit field will lead me into oblivion. Everywhere I look, the shadows tease my senses, overwhelming the brilliant sky with the blackness from the stars, and now the blanket of white drowns the sea of green.

Another hour has passed, another day grows short, and the cold leads to shivers with the thought of your touch, but a dream. I know you are out here somewhere. Are you cold? Shivering? Please wait for me, and invite me into your heart. I fantasize of the time when you will open the satin depths I want to call home. The thought of the eternal warmth of our love is leading me into temptation and I know the scarlet river that harbors forever awaits my arrival. **(Click)**

IV

Such powerful words and meanings, I hope that one day I can again experience a love like that. Knock, knock, knock... That's my door! She's here! I'm sorry, but I must cut this short, I don't want to keep Miss Natalie waiting. Please, wish me luck. I am sure I am going to need it tonight.

CHAPTER NINETEEN

"GO YOUR WAYS, AND POUR OUT THE VIALS OF THE WRATH OF GOD UPON THE EARTH..."

NOVEMBER 7

It's a beautiful day outside today, and better yet, I feel so alive inside. I honestly can't remember the last time I felt this good, let alone pulling up to the computer before dark. I guess these new drugs are working or maybe it was the time I spent with Natalie last night. No matter what it is, I am extremely motivated today, and I want to get back into this project.

I am a bit worried about Natalie though. I don't know what to think or expect right now. Overall, I believed that our date went better than I would have expected it to go. We had a quiet dinner and a couple of drinks at this local Italian restaurant, and we followed that with a trip to the local theater to see an adaptation of *Clue*. And no the outbreak did not come up once during our evening. Although, we did have an interesting conversation about Monsanto and the devastating effects of their GMO (Genetically Modified Organism) based crops.

GMOs are such a great subject to discuss, and unless you have been living under a rock, you should know how controversial they are. Natalie is concerned about the mysterious mass execution of bees across the globe. If you have not heard, bees by the millions are unexplainably dying off with the only viable connection between the location and the deaths being Monsanto GMO crops. I'm not joking; this phenomenon is so sad that some countries have banned the production of GMOs and went as far as barring Monsanto from distributing their seeds within their borders.

At this point, you may be asking why you should care. That answer is simple; no bees equal no pollination, and no pollination equals death. Consider that for a second and think about the outbreak that I am documenting. Did you come up with anything? I did, a certifiable link between Monsanto and the globalists' population control agenda. Did you see it? I should be quite clear.

Sorry about that, I think I am beginning to ramble off topic again. Just believe me, it was an engaging conversation that was certainly in my wheelhouse. I was just a bit surprised that Natalie wasn't at the clinic today. Last night, she said we could make plans for our next date after our group session. Hopefully, she wasn't just cordial, and I screwed something up during the evening. It has been quite some time since I was out on a date and I guess it could be a possibility. I wonder, was I too shy? Or is it feasible that she just doesn't like me? I hope that isn't the case.

I think that this would be a great place to visit Gabrielle and her unborn son Eli. When we last saw her, she was about to take a much-deserved nap. I wonder how that went. I hope one of the foul beasts did not stumble upon her hiding spot.

I

February 15 (Continued),

Baby, that was such a great nap. I don't think I have slept that comfortably in a long time. I know we both needed that to help replenish our energy during these dark days. I would have probably slept longer, but your tumbles and kicks woke me from a dead sleep. Plus, I was starving. Unfortunately, I found out that we have a problem. As I walked through the house, I discovered that there is nothing here for us to eat. Well, at least for me to eat. There is absolutely nothing here, nothing at all!

I can't believe this is happening to us. We finally find someplace where we can be safe from these beasts and there is no food. What are we going to do now? I did take my vitamins, but I imagine you figured that out with the way you have been kicking all morning. Even now, as I write this, you are beating my insides up. At least I have a few vitamins with me, so you will be able to get some nourishment while I figure something out.

What should I do now Eli? We are safe here in this house, but I have to find some food. I won't last long if I don't, especially eating for two. All I know is that the longer I sit down here writing to you, the less motivated I feel to leave this place. What should I do? I know I need to eat something, I know I need your father. I just don't know what to do. Just the thought of dealing with these creatures petrifies me.

*I think I am going to try to get a little power
nap in so I can think. It's funny; it seems as though
my best ideas come to me when I nap, something
that you have certainly helped with. I find myself
napping every day since you were conceived. Wow,
you are much more active today than usual, those
kicks are brutal. At least one of us is having a good
time today.*

II

I have to say, that would suck! I don't know what I
would do if this happened to me. What are the odds
that you would escape the city and find a haven from
these beings and then discover there was no food?
Talk about fucked up! I would die. I love food; I love
to eat. By the way, snack cakes and cookies are my
biggest weakness if we ever meet outside these pages.

I am starting to worry. I still haven't heard from
Natalie. I know it has only been a little over 17 hours,
but still, I hope this is not a sign of her feelings
for me. I did enjoy our date last night and had
been planning our next date all day. I am probably
paranoid about this; she is likely to be busy with
work. I mean, she did come back to the apartment
after the play last night for a drink and stayed until
around midnight. Oh well, I am sure I will hear from
her at some point today; at least, I hope so.

Speaking of women, I think I will jump back
into the story of out another feminine hero. I am
interested in hearing what happened to her after
her encounter with those militarized forces. I guess
I left off with her in quite the predicament. From
the rest of her accounts, she seems pretty resilient; I
would bet she was able to pull something out to keep
herself safe.

III

Holy shit! What did I just witness? Did those bastards in that security force really just kill an innocent? I so hope that they are gone. I want to get the hell out of here, but not if those butchers are still out there. I want no part of them if they are still here or in the area. Damn it; they are still fucking out there. What are they doing? It almost looks like they are inspecting the perimeter of that building where the wasted that woman. Fuck, what are they doing? What is that man telling them in that formation? No, they can't be. They aren't clearing that building; they are dowsing it with gasoline.

God no, how many more people are inside? Fuck, they are burning that building. Oh my God, the cries. The screams coming from inside that building are deafening. What are these bastards doing, those people didn't do anything, and they weren't infected. Who gives them the right? Who are they? I still can't make out what that emblem says. I have to find out, and I have to let the world know what I witnessed here today. They can't get away with these atrocities. We are citizens, and we have rights. What the fuck? What am I going to do now, I have to find a way to escape.

Esther, I wish you were here with me. You always had a way of keeping me calm in the darkest times. Damn, I could use some of that strength right now. My pulse is racing, sweat is pouring off me, and I am becoming dizzier with every passing second. I have to get out of here soon. I need bullets; I need my medication. You know how I get when I run out of my pills. I feel alien, and it makes me uncomfortable inside my skin. It makes me want to kill myself. I just can't stand it.

Why won't these bastards just leave, haven't they caused enough destruction? It looks like they are stalking someone. At least they haven't made their way toward this building. I don't know what I would do if they did. All I do know is that I have to get the hell out of here and would rather face a horde of those vile beasts than this security force. I should find a place to hunker down and hide; maybe they will be gone soon.

IV

Burning buildings, what the hell? We never even entertained the thought of inflicting such damage to our enemies during the war. We tried to minimize casualties as much as possible, especially innocent civilians. Now, I do understand that some of these techniques were used in Korea and Vietnam, but that was a different age with much different technology. Insanity, it is just insanity, although, it does make sense in some ways if the United Nations are involved. Think about what I mentioned earlier about Monsanto and the globalist agenda. The secret shadow government will sink to any depth to reach their population control goals.

As I have said many times, people need to know what their government is involved with and the amount of danger we face on a daily basis as long as the global cabal are pulling strings with the establishment factions inside Washington DC. Incredibly, I can relate to the globalists' desire to meet a goal or deadline. I want to finish this project, and I promise I won't let anything stop me from reaching that goal. At least it seems like I have distanced myself from the visions and voices that were tormenting me early in this endeavor, now it should be clear sailing.

Look at the time. It has been three hours since I got home and started working, and still, nothing from Natalie. I hope she is all right. Maybe I will break down and call her after another entry. Yeah, I think that sounds like a perfect plan.

(Click) *I still cannot fathom what has happened to me. Just a few days ago, I felt alive. Today, I just don't know. I stand, I smell, and I touch, but everything is different. What is the disease that ravages my body? With every step, I can hear the faint crackle of my withering bones as they begin to disintegrate from this unforgiving poison devouring my body. Am I human still, I feel no pain. Is there anything I can do to free myself or make you want me again?*

As I cross this desolate field, tears of loneliness flow from my empty heart. All that can be seen is a weird creature in search of flesh. No one understands the anguish or the memories of happiness. No one can see that my beloved companion eludes me, or let alone acknowledge my soul. No one cares if I have feelings, or if my sanity wavers inside this rotting host. I did not ask for this. I don't want to be a monster. I want to wake from this nightmare and be by your side.

Still, with every step I take, these strange cravings build inside my entrails. My mind remains consumed by the thought of your pale skin lying next to mine. I want to feel you near, but deep down I know the harsh reality that awaits me. You could never embrace what I have become, and our love will be forever forbidden inside this harsh world.

The eyes, stop, no, the eyes, why must they torment me? Why are they fixated on only you? I can sense there are others nearby; their screams echo as the howling winds of misery grow. I don't want to consume them; I only want to consummate us. Gabrielle, I pray that you will eventually forgive my immoral deeds and one day embrace my darkened soul. **(Click)**

V

What love, I wish I could feel love like that again. Who knows, perhaps someday it will happen. What, is that my phone? Could that finally be Natalie? I will keep you informed.

CHAPTER TWENTY

"REMEMBER THEREFORE FROM WHENCE THOU ART FALLEN, AND REPENT..."

NOVEMBER 9

Sorry, I didn't return last night, but I couldn't muster the energy. I was so excited when my phone rang; that the disappointment that I felt when I discovered it wasn't Natalie devastated me. I should have been excited; it was the lawyers' office reminding me that I had an appointment concerning Renae's estate. Unfortunately, my prayers weren't answered, and I wasn't able to hear her voice. I even broke down and tried to call, and her phone went straight to voicemail.

It is so strange; no one has seen her since our date. I sure hope she is all right. I even stopped by the coffee shop she hangs out in this morning, and guess what, none of the regulars had a clue to her whereabouts. They all figured that she had come down with that nasty flu that is going around. I will say that I found her coat next to the couch as I cleaned today, so maybe she was feeling a bit feverish when she left the other night. Hopefully, that's the case, and she is just at home lying in bed.

I don't know, should I run past her apartment and check on her? Possibly, bring her some chicken soup? No, not yet. I will just try to call her again later if I don't hear from her. Yes, the flu, that has to be it. Our date went too well for me to be overly concerned; plus, there is no way she would write me off after just one night, we have become close friends and great partners during the group sessions. She is such a positive person, she may decide to turn her back on our relationship, but she would never do that to the group.

Enough about that, I found some interesting data earlier today. On my way home after visiting the clinic, I swung by the courthouse to see if I could find some information. As I was thinking the other night, it dawned on me that the local budget is in public domain and we have the ability to inspect it at any time. I wanted to check it and dissect the purchases made by our law enforcement agencies over the past decade. This report could give me the evidence that could connect that armored battalion to our local authorities. Guess what? I found absolutely nothing that came close to the purchase of this type of vehicle.

That does not mean I didn't find anything. While I didn't find any specific data for our specific district, I did find an interesting receipt of transfer for multiple police utility vehicles between our police department and a rural community to the south, Summit View. Ironically, this transfer occurred only days after the outbreak. You can verify this for yourself, as I will pot copies of all of these documents on the blog.

Of course, these questions beg the question, why Summit View? There is nothing there. I was out that way a few months ago, and all I found was the remnants of a dying community with almost as many bars and churches as citizens. Trust me, Scotereo's war on coal has taken a huge toll on this town, and it doesn't appear to be a community in need of multiple police utility vehicles. Hell, they barely need a police car.

As of now, I plan to make a trip down to their courthouse in a couple of weeks to see what I can find. I guess with the combination of their rural location and their proximity to some major highways that connect Pennsylvania and West Virginia. This could be a prime location for the government to hide a FEMA (Federal Emergency Management Agency) Reeducation Center. With the devastating opioid pandemic plaguing our area, the actual purpose of one of these camps can be disguised.

Sorry if I seem to be rambling again, but I am apprehensive about Natalie. For my entire life when I forced into a difficult time, I tend to throw myself into some project to help prevent my mind from becoming cloudy. What isn't cloudy though are the visions of pain and anguish suffered by those I am outlining in this manuscript. I wouldn't wish that on my worst enemy.

Speaking of anguish, I wonder if our religious leader has cleansed any sinners since we last met.

I

As Samael yawns and Prometheus smiles,
The eternal breath of forgiveness draws near.
For through the blood, and a defiled canal,
The lone flick of salvation stirs,

And the souls of Legion cry out.

(The Revelation of Moloch *10.1*)

Can you smell the heavenly scent of sin? It surrounds us and fuels our pilgrimage within the depths of depravity. As told by Thy Father, who spoke to the angels as the mortal's shook, our time for deliverance draws near.

As I walk beside you, I am humbled by your deeds. Through your touch, many blasphemers have found their way to the light. And inside that light, they have become one with Thy Fathers' Wisdom. Yes, the nation of sinners may rise against us, but we are strong. We are the Calvary of the Lord our God, and in his name, we will push forward and bless them with the blood of the lamb as we grant the evil ones a stairway to paradise.

The rays of sunlight guide our journey. For across the sky, a blessed sign leads us toward the manger where our destiny waits. Follow this sign and prepare yourself to receive all the glories chronicled in the Halls of Mercy that stand before you. Just as Lilith spoke to Adam in the garden and the serpent dined upon the tree, our path is line with the sweet nectar of Forbidden Knowledge, and with this divine Wisdom, all prayers will be realized.

Thy Father appeared to me in a vision. The womb of our host widens, and the Savior prepares to ascend to his throne. We must ready ourselves for the final conflict; for when the sands empty the glass, the chosen one will rise.

Let us pray.

Lord of Light
Bless those among us who waver in the face of sin
For through the dismay, their absolution is near
Give us the power to stand tall
in the face of the enemy
And illuminate the blood-soaked torch of salvation
Our passage is clear and our mission just
And your son awaits our embrace
In your name, we pray
Amen

I

I have to admit that this situation with Natalie has me a bit bummed. For the first time since I started working on the manuscript, I struggle mentally with conveying a character in the proper context. Nothing I did would allow me to relate to our holy man. Usually, he is the easiest character for me to work with, for some reason it feels like we share some connection.

I don't know what to do. I have called Natalie four times now, and every time it goes straight to voicemail. I keep telling myself to leave it alone, but inside I feel like I should go to her. I can feel that there is something very wrong with this entire situation. Incredibly, I had a similar feeling just before Renae was violated by those puss-filled mutations and I don't want to experience that again.

What should I do? I know I wouldn't survive if I lost her like I lost Renae. I know things are different, and we are nowhere near as close, but still the pain is there. No, what's that? I knew this was going to happen. I could feel it building inside of me. I am going to have to find my pills. I can feel one of those headaches pressurizing my head. I'm so afraid that those hideous voices will return when the migraines come back. I can't handle that right now. The screams, the laughter, they will drive me insane. What the fuck am I going to do?

Pills, I must find my pills. I'm sorry, but I am going to lie dawn and listen to the video from our scientists. If all goes well after I find my pills I will be able to come back to the computer tonight. Plus, I know I would feel much better if Natalie would just call.

II

All right, I'm back after taking a short nap and feel much better. I love this medication and how well it works. This is the first drug they have tried that has kept the visions and voices at bay. Still nothing from Natalie though, I decided to call her when I woke up from my nap and again her phone went straight to voicemail. After I finish with the scientist tonight, I am going to run to her apartment again. I just hope she is there and opens her door.

III

(Play) Thanks, Mark, for letting me finally get some rest, I needed that. It may not have been the best nap I have ever taken, but it worked. I really could not get comfortable with my mind engaged in our quandary. For the life of me, I still cannot comprehend why this has happened. The chemical reactions we are witnessing make no sense to me at all. I have tried, but I cannot understand why there is such a random physiological mutation when this drug combination exists. Not to mention the mental changes, which are even more troubling.

How could these chemicals lead to cannibalism and walking death? From what I can tell, there is no rational explanation for what we are experiencing. Yes, I know that at our core, we are all animals and our pallets have been modified over the years; and because of the recessive nature of our genetics, at one time our ancestors probably prowled the Earth in a manner much closer to these beasts. Hell, even today in some remote lands deep inside rain forests, the inhabitants make what we are observing seem commonplace. Well, at least the craving of flesh. The rising dead are something very different.

To me, that is the symptom that we have to isolate. If we can discover why they are reanimating than maybe, we can find a cure. I know what I am about to say might sound crazy, but we have to capture one of those creatures for our tests. Of course, we cannot do that here in this crypt. I get the proper results I think that our only choice is to return to our lab inside the city. I wish there were another viable option for us, but I cannot think of one.

I know Mark, there is another fully stocked emergency lab in Summit View, but it would take too long to get there. How would we make it the 40 miles on foot? Especially considering we would have to fight our way through that undead horde. I do not know about you, but I would rather take my chances inside the city. At least in town, we are familiar with our surroundings and can quickly move place to place. Plus, with our credentials, we may find some law enforcement officials willing to help. I hope you agree with me. We have to decide something; there is no way we can run a test within this tomb. **(Stop)**

IV

Now that is a predicament, Summit View, or back into the city. Personally, I agree I would take my chances with the city. It would be a rough trip out of town without a car even if those creatures were not stalking you. I will tell you, some of the backwoods folk in that region will in some ways make you believe those beasts we encountered seem like an evolved species. That is a region you do not want to be lost in.

I am going to have to venture back into Summit View in the coming weeks. There are too many connections popping up between my research and now the manuscript. There has to be some type covert government facility in that area that may have some more details about the origin of the epidemic that hit our area. Now, all I have to do is find it and the evidence that could bring our entire ordeal into the open.

I am going to stop here for the night; I finally have prepared myself to check on Natalie again. I sincerely hope I find her safe and sound in her apartment. She has to be there, I mean, where else could she be?

CHAPTER TWENTY-ONE

"AND NO MAN CAN SHUT IT: FOR THOU HAST A LITTLE STRENGTH..."

NOVEMBER 10

Last night after I finished writing, I decided to head off to the coffee shop and grab our friend Janet and take a trip to Natalie's apartment. When we got there, we found nothing of interest. We even asked some of her neighbors if they had seen Natalie. Even they were perplexed by her absence. It has come to a point where we are all starting to worry; there were absolutely no signs of life.

On our way back to the coffee shop, Janet and I discussed reaching out to her family, or even calling the police, but decided to give her a couple more days to show her face again. I honestly don't think that is a wise idea, I know something is wrong, and she may be in grave danger, but against my best wishes, I agreed. I just want to find her; I just want to hear her voice again. I miss it. Yes, I know we only went on one date, but I would see her almost every day, and she always knew what to say when the voices would grow louder.

I received some bad news when I go home as well. The medication that has been a miracle cure has seemed to run its course, and the nightmares and voices returned after a few weeks of sanity. Not only couldn't I get comfortable and sleep, but the countless bouts of crying and screaming were also echoing through the house nonstop. Around every corner, the shrieks begged for help, but there is nothing I can do. I cannot help those I cannot see. There is no way for me to reach into my mind and ease their pain, or rescue them from the torturous cell that entraps them. No matter how hard I try, all I do is fail.

I did receive an interesting package today my friend Dave in New Jersey. We spent some time stationed together at an airfield and became rather close. At this point, Dave is the only person to see what I have completed with the manuscript, and he made a connection within one of the passages from our holy man to a man named Joseph. At first glance, I assumed that the reference to Mary and Joseph were biblical, but Dave believes there is something more modern afoot. He suggests that Joseph is referring to the diabolical NAZI scientist, Joseph Mengele.

I know at some point I drew a connection between our scientist and Mengele, but that was somewhat in jest. However, with the declassified FBI documents showing that Mengele escaped Germany and lived his life in South America being monitored by the government, would it come as a surprise to anyone if they consulted him on any of their Deep Sate experiments? If you look at this in historical context, the trail of CIA sponsored human experimentation did not start until well after World War II. You guessed it, not too long after Mengele (and Hitler) escaped to their South American paradise.

Incredibly, there has been a ton of movies that have dawned the screens in recent years that have also made a strange connection between Mengele and the undead; I wonder if Hollywood is trying to give us a hint. It is a known fact (at least it should be) that government agencies manipulate certain aspects of theater to match the agenda or subliminally educate the population on an individual topic. Don't believe me? Just watch television and pay attention to how the mainstream issue of LGBT rights has been sprinkled into almost every show on all of the traditional networks. Could this be one of those cases with all of the NAZI zombies in games and movies? As I have said many times, I don't believe in coincidence.

I guess it is time for me to stop rambling and return to the task at hand. Where was I? I suppose we could see how our angel Gabrielle is holding up without food.

I

February 15 (Continued)

Baby, I really can't take it anymore, I am starving. As much as I hate to tell you, we must leave this house and head out into that wilderness and find some food. If something were to happen to us after I leave, I hope that you will survive and understand that what I am doing in a few minutes was for you. While I have taken the vitamins that keep you healthy, I have to find some food so I can continue to push through this ordeal and lead us to safety.

I don't know what to expect when we step outside. Before I sat down to write this, I did look across the landscape from the upstairs windows and didn't see any of those creatures wandering through the fields. Hopefully, that will make our passage to the main roads a touch safer. I doubt it, though; I can't imagine that all of those beasts just disappeared (and I am sure they are hungry as well).

If I have my bearings straight, if we hit Route 18, there will a few stores about a mile up the hill. I think that there is a grocery store up there that would take care of all of our needs with both food and vitamins. Who knows, there may be some other survivors as well, and if we are lucky, maybe your father. I miss him; I miss him a lot. It is hard to explain to you in these pages, but my heart aches without him here. I want to feel his warmth, and that sweet caress or peck on the cheek that soothes me when I am down or upset. Damn it, I am starting to get emotional, and I can't afford that as we begin the next portion of our journey. Stay strong Eli. I love you.

II

I feel sorry for her, the nightmare she is living through should not ever be experienced by anyone. The amount of pain and stress she is under has to be immeasurable. I have no idea how I would react if I were there. I would probably just give up; I know I am nowhere near as strong as she is.

Now that I have checked in on Gabrielle, why don't I change directions and add an entry from the man searching for her? While his misery runs deep, his dreams and desires could in no way be as terrorizing as those being experienced by Natalie. Sorry, Gabrielle. I guess my mind is compensating for the pain I am feeling right now not knowing what is happening to her.

(Click) *Gabrielle, where are you my darling? I can feel you close to me, as your scent is forever engraved into my body and soul. I know we have not spoken, and my disfigured reflection will appall you, but the emotional bond and passionate desires we share will deflect all of my dreadful imperfections. With you, I know that our souls and bodies can combine as one and form an everlasting bond that can help is navigate through society and all of the confusion.*

I know when I look into your eyes; I will see a piece of happiness that only you can harvest from within my heart. The eternity we share will not be overwhelmed by questions, and it will be spent together inside a reality shrouded in love. I had never felt this way before and never understood that possibilities that can exist, but now everything is clear.

Inside my mind, I can picture you in the distance where the once quiet streets are littered the revolting remains of innocent flesh marinated in the blood of the unforgiving. Yes, I am guilty of assisting with the spread of these atrocities, and I do long for the taste of your flesh, but I am not a monster. I know I can find the sweetness in your lips, and with that purity locate the clarity that I have been craving. Until the moment when we can be together, these thoughts and feelings will remain bound by who we are and what we have become.

Soon, Gabrielle, all our dreams will be answered. I will hold your beauty close and watch my emptiness vanish along with the loneliness that once defined me. Please stay safe until we can meet. I could not live another day if someone else consumed you. **(Click)**

III

Wow, the emotions inside these accounts today are too much. As I sit here, I can honestly say that I may have never felt feelings such as these. If I did, I can't remember them. I hate to say it, but between surviving multiple tours in the war and this plague, I have almost entirely lost the ability to feel anything. That is one of the reasons I am so upset about this situation with Natalie. For the first time since the epidemic, I started to feel alive again.

I hope that someone hears from her soon. I know we are all worried about her and just a small sign could go a long way in easing our fears. Maybe I should call Janet and see if she heard anything today. I just want to know if there is any change in the situation. Who knows, that may hold off the night terrors that I am sure will torture me tonight.

Speaking of nightmares, I wonder what is happening with the other woman in the manuscript. I think when we left her, she was somewhat trapped in an apartment hiding from some rogue hit squad killing everything in their midst. Did she escape their presence? Or is she still in hiding?

Thank God! Those bastards are gone. Now, I must find my way out of here and find some stores that could help restock my supplies. I'm pretty sure that at the top of this hill there is that plaza that could have everything I need. Damn, I hope so. I would hate to run into any of the bastards out there (alive or undead) in my current capacity.

The streets look clear. I can only hope that they stay that way. Once I get started, if I stay close to the buildings, I may be able to hide if someone or something approaches me. Two bullets, what the fuck can I do with two shots? Well, at least that would be two of the beasts that meet their maker. The real challenge is those men in the armored vehicles. What the fuck was that? I still can't place their insignia. I want to say it is Ravenwood, but I know that is from that show Jericho.

You know, if you replace the undead beasts with nukes, then would we be living in a post-apocalyptic state like outlined in that show. It definitely should have stayed on the air, that brunette was hot. Looking back, it probably hit too close to home with the information it was providing. Those men, though, they seemed something right out of fiction, burning innocent civilians without remorse. What the fuck has happened to society?

I am about to start making my way up 18; I sure hope things stay clear. I don't want many more surprises. I don't know how much more I can handle. I need my medications, and I need more bullets.

IV

Well, that is about where I call it quits tonight. I held out hope for the past few hours that Natalie would call; guess I am not quite that lucky. Good night everyone, I shall return at some point tomorrow with an update, and hopefully some good news about Natalie.

CHAPTER TWENTY-TWO

"BEHOLD, THE TABERNACLE OF GOD IS WITH MEN, AND HE WILL DWELL WITH THEM..."

NOVEMBER 11

I decided to skip group today at the clinic and make my way down the road to Summit View. I didn't feel like spending another afternoon at the facility without Natalie being there. Luckily, I finally found a place to sit down and relax before making the trek back into the city. This may sound hard to believe, but this area is even more rundown than I described in some of our earlier chapters. Put it this way; downtown Summit View looks more like Tombstone than a county seat.

The real surprising events of the day took place at the courthouse, where I found absolutely nothing to help prove the validity of the claims I have documented or unearthed in research. There is no documentation on vehicle transfers or governmental purchases taking place in any of the last few decades. The most recent property transfer took place when the state claimed eminent domain to build the bypass highway just outside of downtown. There is just no connection to be found between Summit View and the city.

I did meet John, an intriguing antique dealer/ historian that everyone seemed to respect. While he could not point me in any one direction for answers, he did have some interesting stories. Incredibly, though, even being only 40 miles away, he hadn't heard about any outbreak in or around the city. I guess that the media blackout was that complete.

He did dive into a piece of folklore that caught my attention. Well, at least it did a great job keeping my mind off Natalie for a few minutes. According to this legend, Summit View has their own Man of Cloth. While I don't readily see a connection between the two religious men, it is fascinating that the Summit View holy man also absolves people of their sins, although his method is by decapitation. True, it is not leading a horde of undead, but the results are the same.

Details about his origins are scarce, with the first mention of his appearance being early in the French and Indian War near the Great Meadow. Unfortunately, there are no historical accounts that can assist in identifying his true identity. I wish there were; I would love to know more about him and where he came from. Maybe when I am done with this project, I will move on to researching this legend.

I just got word from some of the people in the therapy group that there is still no word about Natalie. I can't believe she just disappeared. I am really worried about her; I know that there is something very wrong with this situation. I just don't have any idea what to do. Hopefully, something changes in the next couple of hours as I am on my way home. With the terrible cell service out in this area, I can guarantee that I won't be bothered by anything or anyone until I reach the city.

CHAPTER TWENTY-THREE

"AND KNOWEST NOT THAT THOU ART WRETCHED, AND MISERABLE..."

NOVEMBER 14

I'm sorry that I haven't been around lately to write, but it has been over a week since Natalie disappeared and there is still no sign of her anywhere. No matter what any of us with the group has tried, we have not been able to reach her. Worst yet, her phone appears to be dead and goes straight to voicemail. A few of us even went and spent some time around her apartment to no avail; it's like she just vanished from the face of the planet.

To make things worse for me, the voices and screams have returned at an unbearable level. I thought that this new medication was working, but over the last few days, the cries have returned with a vengeance. Every time I sit down or try to relax, the shrieks echo through my mind. It's so bad that I swear I can hear Natalie's voice within the chorus inside my head. Unfortunately, it's not just the voices that have returned; the bloodstained visions of distress and suffering have come back as well.

Every time I open my eyes, I see those beasts gashing the flesh of an unwilling victim, their teeth tearing into their bodies. The blood, intestines, and gray matter shredded like paper in a mill. Oh, God Renae, look at the way their claws tore through your abdomen, your precious blood flowing like a stream into the rusting drain in the deserted street. No matter how hard I try to push it away, I can still see your lifeless pale eyes staring into my heart. The pain, the anguish, I'm so sorry!

Oh God, please, I can't take much more of this pain. Natalie, I need you. Please come back to me; I can't stand being without you, and I don't think that I can bear the thought of losing anyone else. I have suffered too much already and lost too many people in my life. I'm lost, I have no one to talk to, and I don't know what to do with myself. Fuck, please stop the screams; God, I beg you, please stop torturing me!

There has to be something I can do to stop this disembodied infestation. I have to find a way to make all of this go away. Perhaps I should dive back into this project and let the words of our victims ease my pain. Writing can be therapeutic for the mind and body, and I could definitely use some therapy right now. In this mood I'm in, I think checking in on Gabrielle would be the perfect choice to combat my terror.

I

February 15 (Continued)

Eli, you are killing me today. You are so active, what are you doing in there, backflips? That's what it feels like. Ouch! I don't think I have ever felt you this way. I hope that doesn't mean you are ready to pop out, at least not yet. Trust me; I want to see you and hold you, not now in this nightmare we are trapped inside. Ouch, another kick like that and it is no more vitamins for you. I need to find something to eat soon, though. All of your activity this morning has drained all of my energy.

Honey, it's bad today. This is already the third stop since leaving our safe-haven at the house. Although this stop was more for safety than exhaustion, I can see someone ahead of us in the distance. From what I can make out, I believe it is a woman. Unfortunately, her movements have been sporadic, and I can't determine whether she's been infected by one of those puss-filled maggots. I wish she would give us some sign or a movement that would give me an idea of what we are up against.

I think she's one of us. The way she is hugging the sides of the dilapidated ruins of this once bountiful community looks strategic and well thought out. I can't get past the signs of economic distress that surround us. Remember that there is nothing more important to a community or family than financial stability. The signs of the collapse here are disturbing, and I can tell you that the windowless buildings I am passing could never provide us any protection if something were to attack. I just hope that by the time you are old enough to read this, the damn recession is over.

Eli, you have me in quite a pickle. Every time I stop, you become even more active, and I feel like I am going to burst. But, you are so damn heavy that it hurts to walk and to run is out of the question. All I know is that I have to keep moving no matter how *bad it hurts. We must continue moving; I need to find some food. I love you, Eli!*

II

Insane, I wonder if the woman that Gabrielle sees in the distance is Morgan. In some ways, that would make perfect sense from their earlier accounts. If it is Morgan, I am sure Gabriele would be a lot safer with her than she is outside alone in the street. Even if there is some hormonal imbalance going on with her, Morgan at least has a gun for protection. Although, the idea of two women on the edge of sanity may not be the best thing for anyone involved; the mood swings alone could be intolerable.

Personally, I know I wouldn't want to be anywhere near them. That could honestly be a living Hell. Of course, suffering through this entire ordeal was basically like navigating through the depths of the inferno. But, even that still sounds more enticing and less painful than being trapped with two angry and emotional women. No, I can't say that, I would gladly deal with all of Natalie's rage if she would return. I will admit that I might not like it, but it would be a sacrifice that I am willing to make. I just miss her and want her to return to me.

(Play) *Mark, quickly turn that corner. If I'm right, that alley should take us up to that abandoned tunnel heading toward the Southside. The side streets and alleys would likely be much safer than staying on the main roads. Plus, the authorities are probably blocking the main entrances to the city and likely wouldn't let us back in. I am sure someone set quarantine protocols.*

Mark, please stop, I may have been wrong about that. I cannot see anything, but that stench is unmistakable. Fuck, turn back; I was wrong, stop! That repugnant horde is here surrounding us. I cannot see them yet, but I can smell them. You see them; I know you can; that's why you are standing there in the street like you are frozen. It is the fear or maybe the realization that we created the monsters that have finally hit home.

Dammit it Mark, run. I can see those disgusting degenerates ahead of us in the mist. We cannot go that way. Come on Mark. We have to go. We must find a different route back into the city; we have to get back to our lab. Please, Mark, they are getting closer. Don't do that; don't kneel. God, that rancid stench is unbearable. Please, Mark, stand up and run. Help me solve this puzzle. I am not sure I can do it alone! **(Stop)**

III

The more I write about that man, the more I am starting to feel sorry for him. It had to be miserable watching all of your colleagues and friends become food for the Gods. Even if he did play a role in creating these monsters, he didn't deserve watching everyone he associated with die. One could argue that he deserved a bullet, but watching his spawn dine on his friends may be a touch extreme. Honestly, if this is justified, what more can we expect from the all-loving God and his deeds.

As strange as this may sound to you, while watching the clip I was reminded of a passage I once heard that was written as a tribute to the late Kurt Cobain and demons he faced. Although this musical genius gave into his nightmares way before his time, his words will continue to influence society forever.

The eyes peer into my silence as I drift,
My mind trapped inside a poisoned void,
I am helpless, hypnotized within
the tainted inferno,
Impaled by deceit and the cravings of flesh-
The illicit desires draw near;
help me line your canvas.

Have me; I'm yours...

The needles guide me through the spiral cliffs,
My mind blind to the beauty
bound inside your womb,
I am powerless,
fascinated by the inconceivable pleas,
Tortured by the darkness,
and the forbidden depths-
The serpent draws near; trap me in your guise.

Take me; I'm waiting...

(M.M. 2015)

CHAPTER TWENTY-FOUR

"AND ALL KINDREDS OF THE EARTH SHALL WAIL BECAUSE OF HIM."

NOVEMBER 15

With every passing day, I am finding it tougher to focus on anything, especially this project. I can't believe how hard it has become for me to buckle down and work on anything. I feel so lethargic inside, all I want to do is sit in my chair and stare at the few pictures I have sitting around. It's a far cry from where I was a few days ago, and I can't stand how it is making me feel.

I imagine that it's my fault. I probably shouldn't have made that trip down to Summit View. Between the disappointment and frustration of not discovering any new evidence for my project and hearing about their legendary Man of Cloth, I find myself falling into a downward spiral of disenchantment. Nothing I have tried has been able to motivate me to dive back into or relate this project. I think things would be different now if I could have found just one small fragment of information, just something to show me that I'm not crazy.

I have thought about things over the past few days and remain perplexed by the fact that there was absolutely nothing in the records. For all intensive purposes, it appears that someone or some agency deliberately removed any and all documentation from the files. I know that I could generate an FOIA request for the data, but that would probably only get me the evidence I already have on the vehicle transfer. Plus, I should be long finished with this manuscript before that would ever arrive (if it did at all). After all, the government may be less reputable than the media, and they are both incapable of telling the truth.

Look at things from that perspective gives me only one choice: finish the project. As things have grown, I have the blog set up to continue my research even after I have this complete. Once this information is out there for the public to consume, I have a platform in place for any new discoveries, or accounts that could find their way to me. As much as I would like to move onto something new after this, I just don't see it happening. This project will likely haunt me until I'm dead and buried, the same way the visions and voices will. I have accepted this fate and the fact that those voices will be my only everlasting companions.

Tonight I am again going to try to focus and dig into the project. I need to dive back into our characters and see what has happened since we last said goodbye. If I'm lucky, I will be able to make it through more than one account (which has become normal lately). I wonder where I should begin. I think that it is time to get back in touch with our holy man and see if he has found the child prophesized by scripture.

I

As the apostles pray at the signpost of the Lord,
A distant scream betrays the Martyr
and a lone blackbird cries,
For the blood of the Lamb is near,
And the final passage to salvation rose in the south.

(The Revelation of Moloch 10.10)

Listen my children; the sands of oblivion have shattered the heavens, and the sacred host calls to us from the mount. We must be strong as we ascend the decaying passage, for all our enemies stand guard. Be naught afraid of the pain we are set to endure, for our rebirth has been foretold in the Gospel. The time to bow before the darkest Seraphim has come, allow the light of his wisdom replenish your soul.

For centuries, The Father has battled these infidels on all shores, for their lies and deceit have poisoned the masses against them. Through the blood of our fallen brothers, an everlasting covenant with the ancients has been forged, and you have been chosen to lead a new generation of disciples into the fiery depths for cleansing. Baptize them in the light and welcome their anguish with compassion.

Look upon the blackbird to the south; his wings will lead us to Babylon where the whore and her blessed Redeemer await our generosity. The sacred messenger of the Lord will not lie, at last, our communion awaits our arrival, and Jezebel cries. Let us pray.

Lord of Light
We bow before thee in awe
The signs of your wisdom is clear
And our pathway finally revealed
We implore you to bless our journey into the den
And announce our arrival to the Lamb
In your name, we pray
Amen

II

That is interesting so interesting, that was the first time I picked up the title of the Gospel, The Revelation of Moloch, I wonder if it refers to the ancient deity worshiped by those bastard globalists who dance around naked at the Bohemian Grove. It would make a lot of sense, there isn't much of a stretch between the child sacrifice at the Cremation of Care, and the search for a chosen child for who knows what. Even though they claim that the faux sacrifice is a symbolic gesture in this theatrical event, it is still hard to believe that many world leaders take part in this type of charade. Of course, the same could be said about Spirit Cooking, but as we found out in 2016, some people think it is art.

I'm also fascinated by the thought of the Man of Cloth in Summit View pontificating scripture to the unwilling sinners who meet his scepter. To this point in the ordeal, our holy man has shown tremendous leadership and resolve, and wisdom beyond his years. As much as I would love for it to be true, I doubt there is any connection between the two men. Plus, I have not heard anything about a weapon or scepter in any of the accounts I have transcribed. I will say that his words were powerful, though.

Even today, years after the outbreak, his words radiate a purity that you don't often hear. To me, it is clear why he had such control over his warriors. They were tough, mission focused, and disciple; they often remind me of my divisions in the Gulf. Even though there are many similarities I can relate to and sometimes miss, I am glad that time of my life has passed. I hated the fact that the Navy wanted to take away who I was, and did their best to create a mindless follower. The Navy was so hypocritical, they preached diversity and then shunned individuality. Not to mention the fact that they became overly politically correct and turned their back on tradition because it could hurt someone's feelings.

Personally, I believe that the rise of political correctness across the United States helped usher in the globalist agenda. Just take one look at the leader of the censorship movement across the country: Tipper Gore. Yes, the same Gore family that is pushing for carbon licenses, carbon taxes, and of course the global warming, no, climate change agenda.

Unfortunately, many in our great nation have lost their way and bought into the rhetoric being spewed by the power-hungry lackeys in the world government establishment. Because of this ruse most of the population fears the government and cannot stomach the idea of standing up against authority, even when it is the only thing that can be done. That is exactly what happened here in our city during this deplorable ordeal. There were too few patriots willing to stand up and fight for what was right, and in the end, the entire outbreak was thrust under the shroud of darkness and was dismissed by the media collective.

Now with a regime change finally upon us, maybe our new president will actually stand up and reverse course from the status quo. Maybe he will teach our nation the difference between winning and losing, and do away with the participation awards that have helped spawn the entitlement attitude that infects us. As hard as it is for some to understand, people have to lose, and they can't be afraid of losing. If you fear losing, you will fear taking risks, and by being afraid, you can never win.

One character that doesn't seem to deal well with losing is Morgan. She appears to be singularly focused and is blessed with tremendous instincts. I wonder if she has found her supplies yet. In looking at the accounts, she has had a rough few hours and has not been able to make it very far.

III

Holy shit there is a God! Fucking Wal-Mart, that's perfect, they should have everything I need. There is a pharmacy, a sporting goods section with bullets and guns, and they have fucking food, and I'm starving. I just hope that it's not picked over. Esther that would suck it was picked over. I really can't believe how empty this parking lot is! Maybe I'll get lucky, and the inside will be as barren as the car park. You know things are bad when the fucking Wal-Mart is empty. I just hope they stay that way; it would make my life so much easier right now.

I do need to stop soon and find my medication. I hope the have the Resveratrol; I have never looked for it there. I usually go to CVS or Rite Aid. I need something soon; I think I am beginning to hallucinate. Yes, I expected the side effects, but they have never been this bad before. I knew I felt odd inside, but these symptoms are no fucking joke. I wish the doctor made me understand everythined instead of glossing over them. It probably wouldn't impact my decision to take them, but I deserved the truth.

As twisted as this may sound right now, in some ways I hope it was only my imagination playing tricks on me. For the longest time, I felt like I was being followed. I could've sworn that I saw someone earlier on the road. Looking back now, the streets appear empty. Finally, the fucking entrance, and guess what, its locked! Fucking figured; that's just my luck.

IV

An empty Wal-Mart, I have heard stories about such things, but I never imagined that it could ever happen. I honestly thought it was just some conspiracy theorist trying to get page views. A little while back, there was a story floating around the Internet from either Arizona or Texas that a few Wal-Mart's had closed and were transformed by the government into makeshift FEMA re-education camps in preparation for martial law after the financial collapse. I think all of us are still waiting for that one.

Although that does sound crazy, in some ways, it also seems entirely plausible (at least the FEMA/Wal-Mart connection). If you look at their public brands, they do seem interconnected in some way. Look at the color schemes used they are almost identical. I know that this may sound like a stretch. After all, the same thing could be said about those two organizations and the United Nations, because they share the same color pattern. And we all know those entities can't be intertwined in that manner, can they?

That is an interesting idea, which leads me to question the whereabouts of our rogue squadron once they left the area near Morgan. Yesterday, our scientists seemed to make some progress back toward the city, and today Morgan made her way in the opposite direction, and there was no mention of this unit. It should make you wonder what ops they have going on and where they are patrolling. This could get interesting with the spiritual pilgrimage in the same vicinity.

I am incredibly thankful that the voices have not come back and I have been able to get back into the story. Ever since Natalie disappeared, they have become a constant reminder of her absence. Don't get me wrong, I want nothing more than for her to be here in my arms, but I am starting to function again, and I love that feeling. Over the past days, we have become reacquainted with the majority of our players. At a quick glance, it appears that Gabrielle's distant admirer is the only one we haven't recently visited. I wonder where he is now because at one time he sounded like he was decently close to Morgan.

V

(Click) *I stand alone along this winding path. The blood and pain are the only things that keep me whole, as the shattered mirror into souls fades into oblivion. It was my doorway to everything and nothing, happiness, sadness, and you. The raging currents of regret that churn plague my profane heart. I long to find you, but your sweet scent fades into the bitter howling winds.*

Flashes of life and love, within these days of despair, haunt every step. The chorus of tears, my ball and chain, flow from my mind like a refrain from a melancholy violin in the chilled night sky. The last fugue permanently etched into my flesh, my feelings alive in the shallow melody of your breath that calls to me.

As I roam, these desolate streets consume the solitary desires of lust I once held dear. Gabrielle, where are you, allow me into your void. I must feel the truths you hold close and the realities you hide inside that beautiful mind. Gabrielle, I do not mean to hurt you, for I know this is something I can never have. I can only dream that my impossible dream will become a reality as I drink your wine and dine upon your flesh. I want you to feel the togetherness we deserve.

With every step, I can tell that you are close to me, waiting to save me. Please, breathe life back into my soul, and help wash away my sins. I cannot help what I have become and beg for your touch to soothe my agony. I am but a tainted vessel lost inside this blackness. Please don't be afraid of me, our destiny is signed in blood, and our torment will be eternal. **(Click)**

CHAPTER TWENTY-FIVE

"FOR THE LORD GOD ALMIGHTY AND THE LAMB ARE THE TEMPLE OF IT..."

NOVEMBER 16

I know that it has only been a few hours since I made the potential connection between our religious leader and the Bohemian Grove cult, and I just cannot let it go. Looking back, I can remember the first time I watched a video of the Cremation of Care ritual after radio host Alex Jones infiltrated the complex and captured it. It was one of the most surreal events I have ever witnessed. Just the thought of the world leaders forging policy at this type of event is unfathomable.

I have found a strange anomaly though between Moloch and the statue worshiped at Bohemian Grove. According to ancient Canaanite texts, Moloch was to be half man and half bull, not an owl. An owl version of Moloch can be traced to the ancient Egyptians during the 11th Dynasty when bull veneration was outlawed, but that appears to be the only time period and culture that observes such a

God. While this change could explain the owl statue being present at the grove, it does not match the ritual texts that have been smuggled out that clearly point to the Babylonian deity Moloch. More research will definitely have to follow.

Although, I will say that the connection between our holy man and Moloch, the Canaanite God of child sacrifice, is becoming less surprising the longer in sinks in. Especially when you add in another connection that I discovered doing some quick research. Do you remember the Tonton Macoutes I mentioned in the brief overview of the real zombie mythos? If you do, you may find it interesting that the Tonton Macoutes were named after a mythological character from Creole lore that kidnaps children and eats them for breakfast. Moloch, Tonton Macoutes, flesh-eating mutations walking the streets, there is absolutely no way this can be a coincidence. There has to be a higher power at work here, and that mystical being is at the foundation of this outbreak.

To me, the practice of Idol worship is not surprising; it has been something that has taken place since the dawn of mankind. Ironically, regardless of the origins of the different deities, the power received from the vigil is held tight within the belief structure. At the Bohemian Grove, it is Moloch, one of Satan's most powerful warriors, for the legendary Knights Templar it was Baphomet, the hermaphroditic incarnation of something long misinterpreted, both deities stand as enemies of the Christian God, and both are shunned by the mainstream establishment.

This opens the door to a larger debate, and a harsh reality many are not willing to accept, as there is no right or wrong answer to the question. The recognized religious structure in many nations follows the Christian path, which is understandable with the ancient rise of Constantine and the creation of what can be looked upon as the first globalist society; one based on Christian beliefs within its cultural path. Because this was the majority of the known world at the time, the cultural aspects spread and the religious norms were formulated with many still in power today.

In some ways, these cultural beliefs and the size of the Empire have caused a significant disconnect with reality. From my research into idol worshiping (especially Moloch) over the past few hours, I have discovered hundreds of creation myths that I didn't know existed that completely differ from Adam and Eve. They are recorded in the cultural history of these different lands and can't be discounted because of words in an ancient manuscript. Yes, many as canon accept it, but does that mean it should be law? Yes, biblical history should be fact for some of society and fiction to others. Unfortunately, many can't buy into this harsh truth. Whether you worship God, Muhammad, Moloch, Lucifer, Buddha, or Baphomet, you are not wrong and should not be treated as such.

Because of that, it should not be a surprise that many of the world leaders have organized to worship the Gods that they believe will bring them power. For centuries, these secret societies have always had a place in steering society. Today, there are many other organizations besides the Bohemian Grove. Between the Bilderberg Group, Skull and Bones Society, The Freemasons, and the modern incarnate of the Illuminati, there are many puppet masters hidden in the open guilty of manipulating society.

While some of the outward philosophies may differ between these groups, the underlying globalist agenda is woven into the fabric of all of them. The truth remains that world domination, power, religion, and greed have been causing strife since the societal inception, and our outbreak was likely just an initial test of a grander scenario. It is quite possible that the primary objective of that plan has not been revealed and it remains compartmentalized within the darkness. All I know is that we should be prepared for another outbreak on a larger scale. Consider this book a warning of what you have in store for you.

CHAPTER TWENTY-SIX

"THESE ARE THEY WHICH FOLLOW THE LAMB WHITHERSOEVER HE GOETH.."

NOVEMBER 17

Fuck, shit, fuck, go away already. Please, I will do anything, just go away and leave me alone. I don't know what happened to me after I finished writing last night. I lie down and boom; it was like a nuclear bomb went off inside my skull. The cries, the screams, all of the incapacitating misery were back with a vengeance, and they won't go away no matter what I try. The medication doesn't work, the vodka doesn't work, and there is no chance at rest or sleep. I am trapped in this lurid trance and feel like death.

I wish I could find-stop already! I need to do something to help me escape this nightmare. I want to be normal. I want to cry tears of joy, not tears of pain. Please God, help me, I beg you. If you are so powerful, why must you fucking persecute me with such anguish? What have I done that is so damn bad that you have forsaken me? I just don't know what to do anymore, especially with Natalie gone.

I still can't understand where she went and why we can't reach her. I need her; I need silence, that's all I ask.

I don't know what to do. My only peace anymore seems to come when I am inside this dreadful world inside this project. For some reason, I have been able to connect with these characters in ways that I never could with those I call friends. Maybe it is the inability for these characters to judgmental or argumentative. Or, it could be the fact that they all have a similar desire to escape with both their lives and sanity intact. Either way, I have come to find some connection or kinship with them, and whenever I am not begging for quiet, I am consumed by thoughts of them.

In many ways, I wish I could have been there with each of them. I could have found a way to help them survive and escape. Perhaps then I wouldn't be stuck here alone dealing with the transcription of their stories and we could be working on this manuscript together. I would have been a great companion with my military background and the extensive combat and survival training I have had to endure over the years. Plus-shut up! Plus, with my enlightening personality and higher intellect, there is no way that anything could have happened to us. Hell, I found a way to survive on my own during the outbreak. My only regret is Renae, but I wasn't with her during the events. So, is her death even-what the fuck-yes, it is my fault.

Losing her is the worst thing that has ever happened to me, but if it weren't for her, I wouldn't be here writing right now. It is the sight of her blood, the visions of her body being torn apart by those creatures that motivate me to finish this project. The world must know how we were violated, and understand the corruption that took place over that period. One person that knows exactly the depths of depravity that was on display is our scientist. Unfortunately, he is out there on his own after another one of his team found themselves as a delicious dinner treat for the resolute horde.

I

(Play) Mark, I'm so sorry. That should have been me out in front leading us back to the lab. It was my idea to leave the shelter and navigate our way back into the city and our lab. I should have listened to you and headed toward the facility in Summit View. If I had done that, you would still be here. You would be alive ready to assist me in finding a cure for this pandemic. I know I have some ideas, but I need help, I cannot do it alone.

I have to find a safer way back into town and our lab. After that last confrontation, I don't think that either the main roads or side streets are safe. I know that there is one other potential option available, but I am not sure what will happen if I decide to go hiking up the side of Mount Washington. I have no idea whether the infected will be in the woods. Hell, I do not even know if there is a path or where it would be. Plus, how treacherous is it going down once I reach the peak. I know the incline is there, but I doubt it is running, especially if the quarantine protocol is in place.

Maybe I should stay off the mountain and head down to the tunnel. If the isolation order has been given by the military or one of the governmental agencies involved, the tunnel surely would be guarded, and the authorities or soldiers could assist me in returning to the lab. Of course, that option does leave me in the open as I am trying to transit down toward that area and I will have very little if any, cover, and that could be a huge problem if I run into a group of those undead cannibals in search of food. That definitely will not end well for me.

I guess that makes my decision easy; I will find a path through the brush and trees and tackle Mount Washington and take my chances with what happens. I definitely think it will be safer and who knows, it could be a bit faster, and the quicker I reach the lab, the closer I will be to a cure. **(Stop)**

II

Now that is something I'd like to see. Can you imagine watching our scientist hike up the side of Mount Washington, all the while being chased by a group of undead flesh eaters in search of food by himself? That doesn't sound fair to me; this man surely doesn't have the skills for this type of setting, let alone the experience of being in combat or fighting for his life. Right now, in my condition, I don't know if I could stomach that type of conflict and I have much more understanding of survival and warfare.

No, please, shut up, please, I can't stand the voices-they are driving me insane; everything I do, everywhere I look they surround me. I don't know what to do about this. I guess I am a lot like the scientist in his predicament; there is no right answer or thing to do. In his case, I'm not sure if he is making the right decision. He may not last very long by heading off the grid. Plus, with his credentials, he may be better off heading down the main road to the tunnel; at least there, he could be escorted back into the city. I know if it was me and I could do anything to miss facing those undead beasts, I would do it.

For as smart as he thinks he is, our scientist must lack common sense. This decision doesn't take the environment into account and that could be even more of an issue for him than the flesh-eating faunas. If he does go through with his attempt to scale Mount Washington, he will be up against the harsh wintery elements. From the videos, the snow is at times blinding, and the wind-chilled temperatures unbearable, and the unforgiving mixture of moss covered rocks and fallen trees in amongst the thick underbrush. And, that is not taking the treacherous descent on the other side into account.

I remember the weather like it was yesterday and there was no way I would have ever attempted something this extreme. It's his life, though, he is the one making this decision, and if his video shows us anything, it's a fact, he may not be the best decision maker out there. If you take one look at how his team ended up, there is a good chance he will end up as dinner for these bastards and be joining the mindless ghouls searching for food.

I know I shouldn't, but I almost feel sorry for him having to attempt to make it back into town alone in a bid to find a solution for his crimes. I'm not sure he can do it alone. Sure, he was able to make some progress with a few different hypotheses in the tomb, but testing these various theories without any help is likely going to be a challenge. I'm just glad I'm not there near him; he's the one that deserved to die and I would do whatever it took to ensure he ended up in the belly of one of his creations and fight to ensure his globalist masters joined him.

Well, enough about him, I am pretty sure he will be dead soon. With his luck, he'll likely either become face-to-face with one of his spawn, or he will be overtaken by exposure. No matter what, I'm pretty sure he is destined to meet his maker. With the scientist in the rearview, where should I go next? It's hard for me to focus, as the voices keep pulling me in all directions and their screams take me into a downward spiral of confusion.

While part of me wants to revisit Morgan and find out what it's like inside and abandoned Wal-Mart, another part of me wants to see how our expecting mother is doing. Did lovely Gabrielle make it to her destination? I hope she did; I can't imagine her falling short of her goal, she seems so focused on it. I'm just so torn about where to go, and above all these fucking voices continue to burrow their way into my brain. They are driving me insane, and I need to do something before I give into the pressure. I guess I have little choice; I need to get back into this so my mind can attempt to function again. I hate being here at night; I hate being alone.

III

February 15 (Continued)

Baby, why are you so happy right now, I can feel you jumping around. Those kicks are killing me. I just can't take much more of those kicks today. You're hurting mama right now with the barrage of twists and turns, and I don't know how much more of this I can take. Plus, I'm beyond starving; I need to find some food soon so I can get the energy I need to take you to safety.

When you read this, please embrace the amount of torture and pain I put myself through to keep you safe. Just joking, your safety is all that matters to me. I know you are special Eli; you are destined for great things. This is the sixth time I have had to stop in the past three hours, and I don't know how much longer I can hold out before I collapse from starvation. At least I do have some water to help keep us hydrated, although the snow can help with that as well.

It looks like our luck may have changed, though; I think I see a sign for Wal-Mart ahead of us in the distance. If that is a Wal-Mart, they would have everything we need to keep us safe. They would have food, probably my brand of vitamins, and there's also a possibility I could get a weapon, maybe a small gun, to help me protect you from those damn beasts that are plaguing us. While I am not a huge fan of firearms, I will do whatever it takes to keep you safe Eli, even if it means turning toward violence.

I just hope we're the only ones in there. I don't want to run into any more of those monsters. So far, today we've been lucky, and have not come into any contact with anyone or anything, and I want to keep it that way for as long as possible. I am worried, though, I did see someone earlier ahead of us on the street. From what I could tell, she appeared to be safe. I know it's hard to explain, but she didn't look like she moved like one of those infected creatures, but you never know until you meet face-to-face.

Earlier, when we encountered them, they seemed like they had some useful intelligence. Eli, I just don't know what we're up against and I don't understand how I'm going to survive much more. Please hold on; I'm sure I'll figure something out to keep us moving and safe. Right now, I don't know what else to do but continue on our path. After I catch my breath and find some energy, I am going to make it to that store and find something to eat. I know I will feel more refreshed then. I have to feel better soon; there is no way I can have the vigor to survive if I don't. I just have to do something soon, I feel like I am going to collapse, my head is pounding, spinning and I'm getting very dizzy.

I also need to find us someplace safe to catch a power nap. Damn, thank you, I swear that felt like your foot was going to come right through me. Please, Eli, hold on inside there, I'm not ready for you to be born yet. Just give me five more minutes, and I will get started again. I promise I will keep you safe; I love you!

IV

There is that Wal-Mart again, and it sounds as if Gabrielle and Eli will come up on Morgan pretty soon. It seems like these two were destined to cross paths eventually. The question that I can shake is if both of these women were talking about the same Esther. The name could be a coincidence, but how many Esther's can exist in the world today? If this were about a century ago, it would probably be a lot more. Personally, I hope it's not the same Esther that could lead to some awkward moments inside this empty store.

On a positive note, it seems that diving back into Gabrielle's story helped keep the voices at bay. At least for right now, my writing helped me help me get through another one of these nightmarish evenings. Hopefully, the screams don't return, and I can take advantage of this quiet for a change. I need to get some rest tonight. I think I have only had two hours of sleep over the past two days, and I know that it is impossible to keep up a pace like that. No one can survive on that type of cycle, and for me, it traps me inside this world of pain and anguish.

The longer I go without sleep, the closer I end up to reliving the wretchedness I felt when this epidemic was running full throttle, and back into some of the most miserable days of my life and I don't want to go there. Unfortunately, no matter what I try to do, I can't escape.

It's time to find my sleeping pills and attempt to build a wall around these voices and cut them off before they can erupt again. It is so hard; they have been even worse lately. Ever since Natalie disappeared, its like they feast on my crippling depression. Everything was getting so much better before she went away, now I am just lost without her to help me deal with my anger and hatred. God, I hope nothing happened to her, don't think I could live with myself if something happened after she left here that night. Please be safe Natalie. I need you to come back; I need to hold you again and continue building a new life together.

**CHAPTER
TWENTY-SEVEN**

"AND FOR MY NAME'S SAKE HAST LABOURED, AND HAST NOT FAINTED..."

NOVEMBER 18

Wow, I feel so refreshed today; it's incredible what a good night of sleep can do. I didn't even dread heading out for my morning coffee. I have to admit; I did get a little scared when I turned on my television this morning. I guess while I was sleeping all Hell broke loose last night across the country, as massive protests overran many major metropolitan cities (including Pittsburgh). At first, I thought I woke up somewhere in the *Twilight Zone*, with the scenes of rage, burning cars, looting, and random acts of destruction overtaking the airwaves.

In many ways, these cities looked exactly like our town during the outbreak, except I didn't instantaneously recognize the masses of undead walking the streets. Fortunately, that wasn't the case, as this was just hordes of brainwashed malcontents likely experiencing defeat for the first time in their lives after years of globalist indoctrination. This is how participation trophies' and social welfare handouts can transform a once robust society. It is a sad day when a large portion of society cares more for the causes promoted by the degenerate reptilian overlords than the well being of our nation.

No wonder the government and United Nations were able to get away with the unrest and unspeakable destruction they caused, neither their sheepish populace nor their subservient media could ever admit they could do wrong. Over the years, I have become used to this common thought. Every time I have to visit the VA Clinic, the government funded mental health practitioners attempt to rewire my brain to forget the atrocities.

These people would like nothing more than for me give up this quest, and give into the pressure and conform to their agenda. They don't want the truth to be known, just as the globalists fear a president that lives outside of their conglomerate. That is something that could bring down everything that they have been working on for centuries. Just as my manuscript can be a beacon of hope for the other survivors battling the demons trapped inside their minds by what they witnessed.

I do wonder how all of this will turn out. President-Elect Alexander appears to be the polar opposite of that walking disaster Scotereo, the extreme progressives, and their bankrolled media cohorts who ran our beloved nation into the ground and are now out for blood. Unless someone backs down, we could be in for a rough few years and potentially even a second Civil War. I hope it doesn't rise to that point, but one never really knows what obstacles will come up. Personally, I am not ready for anything like that to happen. I have seen enough death and destruction to last a lifetime.

Speaking of death and destruction, our lover boy seems to have realized he is destined to spend eternity in Hell. I wonder, aren't we all sinners doomed to spend our afterlife in the pit of eternal damnation? I am also prepared for that, after all, no almighty God would be this generous with his torment. He wouldn't stand for the slow death being forced on his followers with the chemtrails, vaccines, and deprived eugenics aimed at reducing the population across the globe. If he were a loving God, he would help fight the infidels and cast the false prophet off his throne upon the seven hills.

Sorry, I can tell I'm starting to ramble again, and I must find my way back into the book. With all this craziness, I imagine the voices in my head are planning a major revolt against my sanity.

I

(Click) Gabrielle, where are you? I count my days through the world in your eyes, although, it feels like forever since I have held you close. I so miss the days when you were sharing my secrets and embracing the possibilities of what could be in each other's arms and the times when words like tears cascaded from my soul. We were not alone, and our bond was whole. Still, I have so much to say to you, and so many desires left unfulfilled.

In visions, I calm. The remnants of your haunting visage soothe my fragile heart and transports to where I can gaze in on the swirling seas of emotion. In those moments, I can again enjoy the slow walks with you by my side on the distant shores of tranquility. I can still feel Heaven in your arms and long for the realities held within that one last embrace. As I look deeper, my mind rips a hole in my heart as my darkest fears turn to blood, and my veins fill with rage.

Through dying eyes, I can see those once pristine sands now stained crimson by the souls of the fallen. My brothers butchered by the unsavory plague and those who fight against the changing landscape of reality. Gabrielle, are you still there? Can you feel my pain? My anguish of being entombed inside this tainted vessel of walking decay, which leaves me spellbound like melting time in a barren Dali masterpiece.

Truths lay before me, for; I am but a memory to you. My body stands as a desolate canvas waiting for a brush or worse, just a phantom voice from the nether. Unrequited? Gabrielle, to me, you are more than you could even comprehend. You are my salvation and my one real desire. I beg you; please wait for me. Allow me to end your pain and consume your divine flesh. For through the moonlight, and the final consummation of love, our forever awaits, and your sacrifice will lead us to eternal pleasure.

Darling is that you I sense upon the horizon? I can hear a faint whisper and pray that your beauty will appear before me. The heartbeat is strong, but the luscious scent of your bowels, though familiar, seems infected with decay. Gabrielle, am I too late? Has someone violated you? I must stop and stand frozen as I await your arrival. Maybe then, at long last, we can finally share forever as one. **(Click)**

II

I wish I knew where our lover boy was in proximity to our damsels in distress. His words, while beautiful, are often cryptic when trying to decipher his location. Out of all of our players, I have no idea when he is from his accounts. I am rooting for him to find Gabrielle and see if there is some connection between the two of them. Plus, from the sound of it, there is someone close to him right now. Could it be Gabrielle or possibly Morgan?

The mass hysteria that has overtaken my television tonight with the insanely biased coverage of the riots is shocking. I find myself mesmerized by the handling of the story. Most of these losers have no idea what they are even protesting, and in turn, they are weakening their cause. Protests can be viable options for change when the messages and voices are unified. Unfortunately, what I am witnessing appears to be organized chaos and destruction in the name of denial instead of an open discourse for the problems at hand. Yes, as a country, we have some issues, but this is no way to address them.

What I see before me is just another example of the failed entitlement generation that believes more in socialism than patriotism. They would rather society distribute their wealth instead standing up and doing their fair share to earn prosperity. These freeloading maggots are content to sit on their asses and reap the benefits of the older generations that understood the meaning of hard work. All I know is that I didn't defend our Constitution for over 20-years to watch these locusts consume our sovereignty.

Who knows maybe those outspoken clingers are right with all of their fire and brimstone and we are early on in the End Times. If I remember right from the last time I ventured into scripture, there was some locust infestation that overran society. I can't seem to remember. I do know one person that has not show a propensity for taking handouts is Gabrielle. I wonder did she make it to Wal-Mart yet.

III

February 15 (Continued)

We made it Eli; we are finally at the doorway. I want to go in, no, I have to go in and find some food, but this door is shattered, and I can hear something inside. I just don't know what to do. I feel trapped out here and I am starving.

Plus Eli, your kicks are becoming more and more brutal with every passing second. This pain has been excruciating, and it feels as if you are clawing your way through my placenta and shredding my stomach lining. Please, hold on a little longer, I can tell you are ready to be free. Are you hungry too? I know I am; I'm starving. I'm just so afraid something evil will be waiting on us inside that store and I could never protect you in this condition.

I'm sure something will notice us or hear my cries. Right now, I can't help you in my state, and I don't want us to end up like those decaying corpses that line the empty streets. I've never seen such terror frozen inside a person's eye. The way those lifeless eyes stare deep into your soul is something I wish I had never seen. Worst of all, this plague is unforgiving, and in no way discriminates against

*anyone. Everyone in its path has been torn to
shreds, and all that remains of their bodies are
ravaged piles of limbs and mangled flesh.*

*I can't believe how the paths of fetid rot
blur the body count. I'm so tired of seeing the
scarlet puddles line the streets with the sewers
overwhelmed by the rotten remains of our brothers
and sisters. I would do anything for this nightmare
to end and for you to be safe.*

IV

Go inside Gabrielle; you will be safe! There is no way
you can survive outside by yourself. I know you are
in pain, but keep moving. You have to keep Eli safe
from those monsters. Oh, wait, what am I doing?
Sorry about that, sometimes I find myself becoming
one with the characters and the dire situations they
find themselves in. This has become extremely
apparent with Gabrielle and her precious cargo.

When I look back, and I often find myself, glad
that I came into contact with her account. She is
such a strong woman, and her story must be heard.
I know there are thousands of young girls out
there starving for a strong role model. Especially
some of those out there protesting today that could
learn a lot from her story and the resolve she has
demonstrated throughout this ordeal. Another
strong woman that could be a solid role model is
Morgan. I wonder if she has found everything she
needs, or at least, found some safety in the store.

*It's a good thing I had some bullets left, one shot,
one shattered door. Now, I just hope that they
have my ammunition in stock. I'll get there soon
enough to see. I have to find some food so I can
finally take some of my pills. If this warning label*

is correct, the side effects could be even worse on an empty stomach.

So far, I haven't stumbled across anyone or anything in here. I can only hope that it stays that way for the duration. Never in my life would I have thought that silence would be so beautiful, although, I would gladly trade this silence to hear Esther one more time. I don't think I have ever talked aloud to myself this much. I wonder if that's why the side effects hit me so hard. It could be that or when I think of it, this is the first time I have run completely out of my medication.

What's that? Do I hear something near the entrance? Maybe it wasn't a hallucination at all; maybe there was something following me. The food will have to wait; I have to find some ammo for this gun. Let's hope they have it. I don't want to be trapped in here with no real way to defend myself. I think its back in this direction.

V

I'm not sure exactly how this is going to turn out. Hopefully, Gabrielle attempts to identify herself before Morgan comes out guns blazing. It would suck if she made it this far only to be mistaken for one of those walking corpses. Especially, since she isn't out there looting like the vultures, I see on the television.

Oh damn, look at the time, I have to stop here and head out to my evening group session. Who knows, maybe Natalie will show up tonight. The day did start off like an episode of the *Twilight Zone*, and I have heard stranger tales. I doubt it; my luck is never that good. I swear that God or whatever our great creator is has it out for me. I have spent too much of my life imprisoned inside a nightmarish corridor that I can't escape, and I doubt that a doorway is anywhere in sight.

CHAPTER TWENTY-EIGHT

"AND THE NATIONS WERE ANGRY, AND THY WRATH IS COME..."

NOVEMBER 19

Stop; please stop! I just can't take this anymore. The voices, the screams, make them go away! Damn you bastards; I don't know anything about the whereabouts of Natalie. If I did, would I be torturing myself? Everything was just fine until early this afternoon when those men stopped me to discuss her disappearance. Fucking soldiers, why are they even interested, isn't this more of a case for law enforcement? You waltz in here in your blue uniforms; I don't understand how you could think that I or any of us had anything to do with her disappearance.

It pisses me off the way they think the can barge in on a group session with no good reason or even an inkling of what they want to find. These pigs are not above the law. They should not be able to intrude on our therapy. We have rights, and some of us have done more in the service of our country than they could ever imagine. Do something to her. Fuck you;

I miss her; she was the only one helping me, why would I do anything to jeopardize that or hurt her in any way?

Shut the fuck up! I can't believe those assholes would toss around baseless accusations and follow that up by questioning my work on this manuscript. How would the even know what I was working on at the house? They must be monitoring me. I wonder if my house is bugged; do they know what I am thinking, or even committing to paper. Snowden was right; they are capturing all our data. This is wrong; the government said they would stop invading our privacy. All I know is that these men had better leave me alone, I didn't fucking do anything. Natalie left this house safe and alive. I don't have any idea of what happened to her; I wish I did.

I'm still appalled at the fact those guys wanted a copy of this book. What does that have to do with Natalie, and if she were their true concern, why would they be interested in it? There are no clues inside these pages to where she is. This book only contains the truth about what happened during the outbreak and revisits some of the lost eyewitness accounts.

Damn you, God, this is your fault. Why should anyone ever trust you or put their faith into your hollow words? How could you have forsaken us down here and allow the tyrants to rage against the devout? I prayed to you, I believed in you, and I defended you at all costs, and still, you turned your back on me and led me further down a path lined with misery.

Who knows, maybe these rich puppet masters are right, Moloch is the way. It definitely seems as if those who follow a darker path are more enlightened all they did to achieve this is turn away from the toxic verse pontificated from your pulpit. I really believe that when I am finished with this book, I am going to search for the Revelation of Moloch and embrace all it has to offer. His words may not lead me astray.

I

Through the screams of the tainted prophetess,
Heaven and Hell awoke,
And the idols cried out in fear,
Repent, for the son of man nears
the canyon of sorrow,
And the loathsome sinners weep as the
almighty Father applauds their damnation.

(Revelation of Moloch 10.12)

Behold, the cries and screams piercing the desolation on the summit. The agony and suffering entwined in the wailing tears marks the blessed altar upon which thy Fathers' chalice will be filled. Be vigilant as our destiny nears, for the final crescendo of prophecy will open the sacred cavern to the gates of our redemption. Our passage has been met with the remnants of oppression and our faith has been tested. Still we have not wavered in the face of the demons, and will continue to baptize the unholy sinners in the blood and the flames brought forth from the valley of despair.

Look not to the fading sun for absolution, for the son of man lay ahead within the womb of the fornicator. Fear not, her disease and wickedness, for the seed of the Almighty has cleansed her of all sickness and depravity. Inside her bowels, the Messiah has at last opened his eyes as he prepares for his journey into the light. Bless his arrival with the sanctified marrow harvested from the festering hosts and make a final sacrifice to thy Father.

Honor his wisdom and precepts with the blood of the martyr rising from the east. This battle will not be easy, as many before us have fallen short of salvation and their souls are forever entombed inside the iniquitous scepter that sits in the right hand of Judas. We must stand tall and profess our everlasting allegiance to thy Father as we crucify the witness upon the oaken cross and set him ablaze with the vestiges of the fornicator.

As was written in the Gospel of Abaddon, we must cast them into the abyss known as tribulation, bind the stone crypt with the flesh of an innocent, and adorn this tomb with consecrated iron spikes in the name of the savior. For through this final blessing, our liberator will rise, and all will know his name. Let us pray.

Lord of Light
Bless our passage into the desolate wilderness
For the signs of the Gospel, appear on the mount
And we fear we are unworthy
disciples of your wisdom
We stand in the face of condemnation
ready for battle
Our prayers strengthen our resolve
And our faith will not waver
in the face of the enemy
As the cries rise from the frozen ash
And one heartbeat becomes two
Grant us the power to stand before your son
and baptize him in the light
For through this Christening
Eternal deliverance will be at hand

And your prophesized rapture will commence
In your name, we pray
Amen

II

What is that? The cries have changed; they are
surrounding me like they are preparing for a mass
or vigil. I wonder; can they hear these accounts? Do
they want me to be their sacrifice? If that is the case,
they better come take me. I would never condemn
myself to Hell by taking a blade to my wrists or a
gun to the mouth. Besides, I have already spent
decades inside Hell trapped here on Earth and I
don't ever intend on going back into the depths.

I can't believe the hopelessness of these voices
today, they are driving me mad with their moans
and sighs. Fortunately, they at least quieted during
my work on the project and allowed me to focus
on that last account. It was probably the extra
attention I often give to our religious leader, I am
always captivated by the black-shirt and his way of
massaging words to fit into coherent thoughts full
of power and might. I feel such a connection to him;
even my personal feelings on life seem to match
some of his thoughts, as I frequently feel unworthy
of following in the footsteps of some of our demonic
elders. As much as I would love to receive the sacred
wisdom, the unspeakable losses I have suffered
continue to ensure my banishment from the depths
of eternal pleasure.

I do wonder about this martyr from the East
that was mentioned inside the account. I really
feel sorry for whoever that is. I have dreamt of the
pain one could feel inside the lake of fire and I can

imagine that the agony inflicted on the believer will be prodigious. I wonder of it could be our scientist; he was preparing to scale Mount Washington, which sits to the east of our current location and there were multiple references to a Mount inside this last account. It's actually past the time that we should have checked on him. I wonder how the latest leg of his trek is going. If his athleticism and luck were anything even close to that shared by his team, the odds are great that he will be struggling with the decision he made.

III

(Play) *I think I see a path down there by the opening in that fence. As bad as I feel for Mark, I am so thankful that I was able to escape from the clutches of those infernal beasts. I do wish he could be here with me, I know that if we put our minds together, we would have been able to come up with the exact remedy that is needed to combat these fiends. Not to mention the fact that he would have been a huge asset in the lab. Right now, I have no idea how I am going to get anything done by myself.*

Fortunately, I am pretty sure that my plan has outlined every test that could assist in finding a solution. I know what data must be analyzed and what type of link I am looking for inside the results. All I know is that there has to be a way to isolate the cannibal tendencies within the genetic code. Maybe I should do an abstract comparison of animal and human DNA to see if there are any major differences. I know there is a link somewhere; our ancient ancestors lived their entire lives with an appetite for flesh.

*God, I hope that I can find something to help us.
I have to find a cure for the disaster I have created.
I do not think I could live with myself if I fail again.
I am also interested to see if there have been any
changes to the rats since the evacuation. Prior to
the onset of the outbreak, there were no noticeable
changes to any behaviors in the test subjects or rats.
Once the human symptoms started to materialize,
we never went back in and checked the other living
specimens to see if the apparent dosage level or
gestation period may have differed between species.
At this point, the answer could exist anywhere, so I
will not take anything off the table.*

*Hello, is someone there? I feel like I am being
stalked. Hopefully, I can make it to the fence without
incident. Hello, I know you are out here. I know
there is something out here; I can feel your eyes
watching my every step. The faint stench of decay
emanating from your shallow breath, betrays you;
I know you are here. I may not be able to physically
stand against you, but I will not run either. If you
are here, show yourself, coward.*

*Oh God, what have I done! No, I am so sorry. Is
that you in that dark silhouette inside the blinding
squall? I am sorry, I never meant for any of this
to happen. Please forgive me, and let me pass so I
can find a cure. Better yet, just stay back there and
I will find a different way to make it to the facility.
I have no desire to cause trouble-stay back, please.
Please don't come any closer, I beg you. Please
stay away.*

*Oh Lord, oh God, I am sorry for discounting you
and your genius. Please forgive me for-no stop,
please no...***(Static-Stop)**

IV

No, not our scientist, he had to survive. No, this
can't be happening, he couldn't be dead. I know,
I must have another SD card here somewhere,
this story must continue. I know I wanted
him gone, and I despised him, and I may have
threatened him, but I didn't want his story to end
this way. Maybe he isn't dead, maybe he has been
captured by that religious cult and he is going to
be sacrificed as the martyr mentioned in the last
scripture.

Somehow, I doubt that's the case. From the
descriptions in the account and the visual evidence
captured on film, the area does not seem to be in
the vicinity of the religious pilgrimage and there
were also no signs of any type of group converging
on him. In fact, from what I could tell it was a man's
shadow breaking through the overcast sky and dense
snow showers.

After all this time, I can't believe he is gone.
Just the thought of his passing pains me, as I saw
no reasonable way on the video that he could have
survived the vicious attack. Even if he was able to
miraculously escape, there is no way he could have
managed to hold on to his test data or research;
yet, another setback to developing a vaccine.

Please stop tormenting me! Go away, I want
to keep working on this. Stop, I beg you. Damn
you, I will have to stop, the voices won't go away.
I was doing so well at keeping them at bay, but
that last entry did me in. It brought me down
to a point where the visions and screams came
together to overwhelm me. Shut the fuck up!
Stop already, I can't take any more! Sleeping

pills, I must find my sleeping pills they may be the only thing that can help me right now. God, no, Stop!

CHAPTER TWENTY-NINE

"...NEITHER WAS THEIR PLACE FOUND ANY MORE IN HEAVEN."

NOVEMBER 20

As I sit here tonight, I am still devastated from the accounts from last night. I feel such a loss inside. As much as I despised that man for what had done, I didn't want to see him go out that way. I really thought that he would be the one that found the cure for this madness. Hopefully, today's account will not cause such an emotional response and I will be able to push through.

With his loss, I am starting to get the feeling that our days together, exploring these lives, may be coming to an end. Trust me, I wish that this project could last forever, but I also realize that I must get this information out there. Plus, as I look at my desk, it is clear that the tapes and notes are winding down and I can only do so much to keep these doorways open. I don't want to leave you, but these accounts must be shared, so the sheep of the world can be informed.

Incredibly, as much as I dreaded this project when I started, I am going to miss every aspect of it once I am finished. Over the past few weeks, I have found some type of connection to all of these characters, as they have basically become my family washing away the emptiness as I sit here. This has been extremely important, especially since Natalie disappeared and I could not thank them enough. The loneliness I feel is something that I would not wish upon anyone. Everyone I have loved has gone, leaving me alone to face society with no real outlets for my troubles. I just hope that I don't experience any more death today; I really can't stand the thought.

I did find it funny today, as the grey dreary skies eventually gave way to brilliant bursts of sunlight. It was like the scientist looked down on me and attempted to dry my tears. That didn't work though. As I opened my eyes, I found a world of remorse mourning the loss of our friend the scientist. Things got so bad that I wanted to escape and turn my back on everyone causing my pain. There was a part of me that debated giving up on this project and moving on with my life. I have lost enough already. First Renee to her afflictions, then Natalie disappeared, and now the unlikely family, which has given me hope, is starting to go. I don't know how much more pain I can handle.

It's hard to explain, but the bond I feel with these characters is so strong and the connection we share is like nothing I have ever experienced. When they cry, I feel their tears. When they bleed, I feel their pain. And, as I have just discovered, when they die, a part of me becomes lost in the abyss that binds us. However, the have also given me the strength to remain strong in the face of turmoil. Deep inside my soul, I realize that I could never turn my back on them and must persevere no matter how difficult things become. I know that's what Gabrielle and Morgan would do, so I much follow their lead and finish this.

I

February 15 (Continued),

Eli, I need your father. Something is happening to me, and I don't know what to do. As soon as I found some food, I could feel you become even more alive inside me. Your kicks, your turns, everything about you was different. Not to mention the pain became unbearable. I know you love when I grab an apple, but this reaction was pure insanity.

I also found you some more vitamins before sitting down to rest. I can't explain it, but I feel so different inside and I'm not sure how much longer things will stay this way. I don't think you will be in there much longer. The pressure in my abdomen is creeping downward. I swear you think my bladder is a punching bag. I just don't know what I would do if you decide it's time.

I still think I hear something in the back of the store. Luckily, I haven't seen any signs of life come from that direction. I pray it is not one of those creatures; there is no way I could keep you safe if one were to appear. I keep holding out hope that it is Isaac coming back for us, but I realize that desire can only be a dream. Dammit Eli, must you continue beating on me? I'm trying my best here given the circumstances and I have no idea of what else I can do to help you. I know

*you want your father to be here, but he's not. I'm
sorry, it's just me and I'm doing all I can.*

*Oh God, Eli, what's that? This moisture, where's
it coming from? Oh God, the pain, nooooo, not yet?
Help make this all stop!*

II

This can't be happening. There is no way Gabrielle
can go into labor at the Wal-Mart. This really may
not end well for anyone. I'm not even sure Morgan
can help with this situation. I know she could help
keep her safe or protect her from the monsters, but
delivering a baby is something altogether different.
This has to stop; I'm not ready to see what happens
to Eli.

With this worse case scenario unfolding, I wonder
where our lone flesh eater is and whether his bond
with Gabrielle is as strong as he has led on. Can he
sense the pain and urgency coming from her cries? I
can only hope so. When we last caught up with him,
he sounded like he was near some type of open field
searching for Gabrielle. I am sure he has moved on
from there by now. But, where could he be?

III

(Click) *Oh Gabrielle, what have I done? My heart
has been shattered by my wretched deeds. I have
tried in vain to stay true to you, wanting nothing
more than to finally consummate our bond by
sharing in the gratifications found each other's
flesh. The thought of your conversion stimulates
every sense in my body. Please do not question my
faithfulness to you with what I have done, as the
aching inside my decomposing void finally seized
control. I hope you can forgive me, as the empty*

visions of the carnal desire blinded my mind as my ravenous innards filled with rage.

In the distance, I can feel you as you lay. Your tears of pleasure and cries of pain called to me, yet, his presence in the falling snow engulfed my sanity. Did you hear the last gasp of sin as I tore into his abdomen and drank from the scarlet streams that line the walls of his mind? He was delicious, and the warm taste of his beating heart upon my tongue was divine. I promise you though, I was gentle, and he only struggled for a moment. But, I will say, the sounds of his screams made everything taste even sweeter.

Inside my dying shell, I can feel the virus calling for more flesh. My once beautiful dreams have faded deeper into the depraved depths I now call home. Why was I consumed by this strange infliction where the once forbidden cravings now run deep? While I can still feel love inside my lifeless heart, my desires are not only for your touch, but for the divine grey you harbor. I salivate at the thought of opening your veins and sharing eternity by your side.

Sanguine tears fall from my sunken black eyes as storming emotions swirl inside the empty passions I hold onto. Forever was once near for us and our bodies perfectly combined as one. We were soul mates and lovers, conjoined best friends with our undying hearts beating forevermore. Why did I fall prey to this unforgiving infection and have God trap me inside oblivion. I know you warned me about the dangers involved, but my stupidity reigned over allegiance, but did I truly deserve this punishment?

Outside the fervent screams and cries of the docile slaves overtake the bloodstained streets that surround me. I can sense it will only be minutes before more sinners close in for a final battle, their minds oblivious to the realities that lay before them. As I wait, my pulse quickens at the thought of my teeth tearing into another beating heart, the pulsating warmth and savory elixir stimulating every gland in my body. My guttural breath hastens at the thought of a life with you by my side. I know, if you are willing to experience the luscious taste of flesh and dine on the souls of the wicked, our love will overcome every obstacle that appears before us. I for one cannot live alone inside these nightmares much longer and I want to again share the memories of your depths, the Heaven along your curves, and the sweetness of your lips. Our reunion is near and I long for our next embrace.

As I stand over the remains of my latest feast, I am torn by the desires I have for you. While I know my life is in ruin, I know my true feelings for you will never die. Will you save me and join me on a forbidden journey into flesh. I know you will if you just let me hold you again. Everything is different now, as my body craves every inch of your purity and nothing more. My eternity can only be found in your arms and until the moment we sanctify our bond, my soul will never be whole. **(Click)**

IV

So, it was you that devoured our scientist! You bastard, why would you do this? I wanted to be the one that found him and ended his life. All right, I may be jumping to conclusions as I have no real proof, but from the audio, it definitely sounded like our scientist when his pleas echoed through the room.

I can't believe what I just heard this recording was brutal. Between the screams and the popping of bones, the entire ordeal turned my stomach. Even worse were the gurgling, the unnatural gasps of putrid breath, and the raucous inhumane growls rising from the depths of the entrails and the pleasure; with every breath an outpouring of passion melding with a frenzied climax that is easily heard through the blowing snow. How could this happen? There is no way these two men should have crossed paths. From the past entries, I would have sworn that our zombie was near the house or the cemetery. From my calculations and interpretations, he should have been nowhere near the tunnel.

It was interesting that he did seem to sense something with Gabrielle. I wonder could the man we have been following be Isaac. I know she has mentioned him multiple times in the different accounts, so I know he is out there somewhere. Plus, the connection that they seem to share seems more than a coincidence and I don't know about you, but I don't believe in such things.

Now with Gabrielle seemingly going into labor, I wonder if Morgan has found her. Here's hoping that she didn't shoot first. With the way, she thought she was hallucinating; anything could be possible under the right conditions, especially if some of the side effects from her medication return.

Damn it, someone is knocking at my door. I guess I will stop and pick up with Morgan when I get back from dealing with whoever is outside.

Mark A. Mihalko

CHAPTER THIRTY

"HE THAT OVERCOMETH SHALL NOT BE HURT OF THE SECOND DEATH..."

NOVEMBER 22

After taking a night off last night in an attempt to drive these migraines and voices away, I woke ready to take on the world and this project. I will be the first to admit that the past few days have been a challenge. The emotional rollercoaster that is taking place within the confines of our story is having a grave impact on my ability to immerse myself into the characters. Between the death of our scientist and lovely Gabrielle going into labor, I am almost afraid to see what is next.

I know I said I would get to Morgan before the pizza delivery guy rudely interrupted me (and it wasn't even for me), but I think I need to veer off into another topic for a moment. I promise, sometime before I finish tonight, I will get to her and see where she is.

That is when I realize that today was November 22, a fay that for many will live in infamy because in many ways it is the day that America was truly brought to its knees by the globalist cartel and the deep state military industrial complex that is in full agreement with the globalist agenda. Today is the anniversary of the assassination of President John F. Kennedy, one of the first outwardly anti-globalist world leaders and a true beacon of hope for America.

While there are many sheep out there, that still believes the story that Lee Harvey Oswald was a lone gunman. The fact remains that there is no way this man could have worked alone to plan and carry out one of the most incomprehensible attacks on United States soil in the history of the nation. Even the Congress sub-committee agreed with that notion noting in a rather obscure publication that there were four shots at the president, not the three (including the magic bullet) contained in the Warren Commission Report. To me, the Warren Report should be filed in the same category as the fraudulent 9-11 Commission Report as globalist propaganda out to brainwash society.

For those that don't understand why Kennedy was dangerous and became a target for the globalist dictators out to control the world, all you have to do is look at some of his public statements and stances that went against once accepted doctrine. Kennedy was the first Catholic elected president and he was more conservative on some of the social issues than much of the more progressive left, he was extremely pro-freedom and pro-liberty standing up against the rogue elements within the CIA and other government agencies that sided more with the globalists that the American citizens, and of course, he had a large distrust of the Federal Reserve and was taking the first steps to rid the United States of their subversive financial controls.

Yes, this may sound like random ravings from some insane writer caught up in breaking down what appears to be a globalist engineered zombie apocalypse, but it is all truth. His brother Bobby Kennedy knew the truth, and attempted to run for president to finish what his brother started and we all know what happened there. Yes, he too met an assassin that snuffed out his life with a bullet before he could achieve his goals. Incredibly, many believe (and there may be evidence) that his murderer, Sirhan Sirhan, was a Manchurian Candidate brainwashed by rogue elements within the CIA and FBI to carry out the deed.

The ongoing cover-up of the truth behind the Kennedy assassination did not stop there. As soon as his son John started to build political capital and hinted at following in the footsteps of his father and uncle, his life too was cut short. In 1999, Kennedy was killed in a mysterious plane crash that still today has more unanswered questions than facts and left America waiting to hear the truth and longing for another family to rise to power and rebuild Camelot.

One of the things that become clear to me when looking into these and other) events and a possible connection to what took place during the outbreak is the underlying presence of the government and their globalist partners. We know from the scientist that he has a background working with both black ops CIA research operations and the United Nations. Our zombie (Isaac?) escaped the World Health Organization facility and from the description, Morgan encountered a United Nations convoy. Why are these agencies here and why do, they hate the sovereignty of our nation?

Maybe someday, we will be able to find out. If our new president has his way, the answers could be coming soon. For the first time since President Reagan (who was also shot in an assassination attempt) and President Kennedy, it appears that President-Elect Trump is against many of the agencies that the globalists use to control societies across the world. If he does in fact stand up to the United Nations and NATO, the elite will not like it and do whatever they can to take back control.

It will be interesting to see how this all shakes out, if the highly coordinated and funded protests that have transformed our streets to scenes from the Twilight Zone are any indication of how these leaders feel, we are in for some long days. I just hope there that more people start waking to the corruption that has seeped into our government and will work to keep them accountable to the citizens of our nation instead of the international spawn looking to complete the construction of the New World Order.

Fuck the New World Order and fuck the globalists they must be stopped! We must all stand up against them and make them pay for what they have done to our nation. Just look at what they did to the people outlined in this documentary of misery. No one should ever have to deal with the atrocities that took place over these dreadful days. No one may have suffered more than Isaac; he was infected and has had to come to terms with the fact he has transformed from a human to a flesh-eating ghoul full of illicit cravings and forbidden desires. I know when I last left off with him; I was a bit out of sorts. I wonder where he is now and if he is against feasting on a sinner.

I

(Click) *With every step I take, I still cannot comprehend the repulsion I feel inside my veins. Everything is so vivid, blinding from when I was a much better me. I remember standing above you before I left that day for the first session. I remember your words, and playing witness to your pain as I left. I have no idea how you could you endure the hurt I put you through.*

The misery that was frozen in your eyes on that day stand as beautiful daggers of despair that haunt me still. Yet, the tranquility of the night echoes within me as a surreal nightmare that will never end. Now my heart cries out as I walk these desolate streets. I must silence the anguish and hope that our secret will remain safe. No one could ever know the bond we shared, or the destiny that we planned. If discovered, my sacrifice will be for naught.

At times, the remorse challenges my resolve by slicing through my soul and filling my void with darkness. I am hopeless, and helpless within this reality that has poisoned my body. There is an unexplainable emptiness that wears on my façade, shredding the fabric of what was and destroying what could have been. No, sadly annihilating what should have been if I wasn't blind to the darkness that surrounded my heart.

Today, I must endure, as all of my thoughts of you entrap me inside the spiraling visage of my incompetence. The way my talons slid across his throat, or my razors tore into his abdomen. Oh, the way the river of sadness that flowed from his veins, it was magnificent. But, it was my lone tear drying upon his skin that shattered my world and woke me to the monster I have become.

I know now lovely Gabrielle that my tears will never dry and my life will never be the same. I once had a love that stood as my foundation, which shaped all that I was and helped me through the blackest days. With that gone, what I have become?

As I stand among the snow, I can feel deep inside my emptiness a strange turmoil rages surrounded by my penitence and sorrow. I am lost without you, without your touch and I often wonder if you will forgive me when we meet again.

Why was it my hands sliced through the flesh? Why am I so afraid of the pain I still feel? I can see these will be questions that remain a just punishment for my failure and a life sentence within this decay. I should have surrendered my body to science and I should have never left your side. (Click)

II

I can definitely feel the emotions inside him. Whether it was Gabrielle or someone else, the love this man shared had to be strong. What would drive a man to make such sacrifices and subject himself to being a lab rat? Was it the economy or something else? I understand that many in America lost hope at some point over the last decade, but these feelings described inside these accounts are depths that are beyond desperation.

I still can't figure out what to think about this man. Is he good; is he evil, or a monster? On one hand, I feel for him and the pain that he has endured being transformed into a beast trapped in Hell on Earth. But, he is also a murderer and a cannibal, dining on the flesh of humans, quite possibly on some of the friends that I lost during the remorseless plague. Part of me wants to hate him, while another part of me wants to save him (if he is still alive).

I hope that we can all stay safe and possibly see these globalist pigs pushed once and for all from our shores. We don't need ancient bloodlines determining who lives or dies, or who are rich or poor. We need to embrace the pillars constructed by our founders and fight back against people like Soros or the Rothschild's.

Speaking of battles, I wonder what Morgan is up to. I wonder if she has found Gabrielle.

III

What the fuck is happening up there? I swear I hear both screaming and crying coming from the front of the store. Luckily, it isn't those godforsaken moans that continue to echo through my head. I can't stand them, or the damn smell. Those creatures smell like shit.

There she is, and she looks to be alone. I wonder what is wrong. Hopefully, it is nothing more than exhaustion and fear. I really don't want to deal with anything more that that right now. I don't think I have the strength and I don't really want to put another life in my hands. We all saw how that turned out with Esther.

Maybe if I can get a little closer without being seen, I can find out some more information before I decide whether I should make myself known. At least now, I have more than enough ammo to keep me safe and I want to keep it that way. Who knows, maybe I'll get lucky and she'll leave before I get up there. It would be nice to keep this place to myself for a while.

Oh God, I don't think she is leaving on her own; it looks like she is pregnant, and, as I get closer, and it looks like she is in labor. Fuck, I can't deliver a baby; I don't even like children. Just the sight of a baby sends chills down my spine and turns my stomach. Fuck, what am I going to do? Fuck!

IV

Well, that sucks. Who would have thought that Morgan would hate children? I definitely think that this part of our story is going to get a lot more interesting in the next couple of entries. I can't wait to get there.

Unfortunately, I can feel a headache coming on and I know what will happen if I don't squash it before it starts. I am going to sign off for now and possibly settle down with an informative JFK documentary. Who knows, I may find some other connection inside that will unveil more truths to the inhuman globalist agenda. I will see you tomorrow night, I hope.

**CHAPTER
THIRTY-ONE**

"HOLD THAT FAST WHICH THOU HAST, THAT NO MAN TAKE THY CROWN..."

NOVEMBER 23

Please stop, I can't stand that screaming, the shrill drives me insane. Where does it come from, why is it here? All I want is for it to stop and go away. I want to be whole again; I want Natalie to come back. I can't go on like this. The headaches, migraines, all of the misery, I just want it gone. Last night was one of the worst nights in my life. It sounded like a war raging inside every heartbeat and breath. I wanted to die. Please, help me end this.

As I woke today, the remnants of the anguish I felt last night was still visible in the mirror. My eyes sunken and my flesh is tattered almost withering toward nothingness. I can see my pronounced cheekbones rising from my skull. This torment is ravaging my body and corrupting my mind. Even at group today, I could feel the stares. Every one looked at me in ways I haven't seen since being an enemy upon a foreign soil. I was an albatross, and if I don't stop these voices soon, I will be gone.

I really thought that as I moved toward completion of this project, my entire being would improve. I figured my health and mental stability would progress toward living a full life without the therapy and drug induced impediments that I swear do more damage than good. I'm no doctor though, and I could be (and probably am) wrong about that. I am probably destined to deal with these monstrosities for the rest of my life.

I have nothing left to live for except my work on this project and even that is working toward eating my mental faculties. I want to finish, but am so afraid that the voices will never leave if I do. This is so miserable and I am starting to see the light before me reflecting off the sharp blade I stare at almost daily. Please leave, let me live. I'm not ready to see the blood again or taste the finality of death.

One group of people that don't see concerned about meeting death is our religious leader and his army that is out in search of their Messiah. I wonder if he has found him yet, or ran into any infidels out to stop their journey toward the promised one.

I

As was written in the depths of darkness,
The wine of the strong will baptize
the first born upon ascension,
Take, drink, this is my blood,
And through this offering, the
young Messiah shall be ordained.

(The Revelation of Moloch 11.2)

Look beyond the fork at the plain of redemption

that lay ahead. Listen to the cries of sorrow echoing among the emptiness held within the barren streets and embrace our reality. Thy Fathers' prophecy is upon us and we must prepare for his coming. As the Gospel decrees, we must preserve the bloodline of the child and baptize the unwilling host to achieve our salvation.

As our journey nears sanctuary, I can feel the evil one approach. Have you felt it as well? This is not the first time that this being has crossed our path, they were there during a sacrifice and escaped confirmation. We must branch out and find the sinner before we can deliver the son to Thy Father. Our redemption cannot be achieved until we imprison this fiend in the heart of damnation and curse their souls to survive eternity like John with their head garnishing the platter upon the altar.

Do not waver in the face of evil, for this encounter has been foretold in scripture and our victory enshrined upon scrolls decreed as canon; just as the tablets of Moses guide the non-believers away from the idols of absolution toward a mirage of pleasure. Stand tall in the face of deceit, and remember that we shall provide the true path toward enlightenment for all, including the non-believers. For through the anguish one of our legions will earn their wings and raise one step closer to eternal salvation near the throne. Let us pray.

Lord of Light
We bow our head in praise
Your words have again provided the guidance
And your deeds have provided the direction
Hear our prayers and watch over us
The final steps toward salvation near

And the final battle lay ahead
As the Martyr comes from the East
A sinner lurks near us
Bless us as we fulfill your prophecy
Allow us the strength to baptize your son
For he is the Messiah and the Savior of Mankind
In your name, We Pray
Amen

II

What intensity found in those words. The depth of
this mans verse and love for his father is amazing.
Maybe he is telling me something; does he want me
to reconnect with the church? Or start channeling
to voices and recording what they are telling me?
Is it possible that the visions and voices are not
nightmares but prophecy of what is to become? If I
remember some of my biblical history classes, that
is what was in the material presented to us. Imagine
that, me a prophet. Fuck that, there is no way I
am a prophet. I am more likely to be insane and
committed in a straightjacket then be a prophet.

As I sit here working on this project, I can't help
but allow the music in my headphones drown out
the voices. When it works, it is so relaxing and it
allows me to make some great progress on things.
Fortunately, that is the case tonight, as the words
and melodies have taken me far from this Hell.
Unfortunately, there are times when the words and
music lead me down a path that I am not yet ready
to revisit.

Lou Reed and The Velvet Underground are one
of those groups. No, not *Heroin*, although that
is a classic, it would never be my drug of choice.

Classics like *Walk on the Wild Side*, *Sweet Jane*, and *Pale Blue Eyes* conjure visions of Renae and the extraordinary journeys into silence we used to take before she was ravaged by the beasts. What I wouldn't do to find a wormhole and travel back in time to save her. Things would likely be much different right now. Now, it's The Cure, a band that has been a major influence on me since I heard *Killing An Arab* all those years ago.

I have to wonder what is going through the mind of Gabrielle right now, I couldn't imagine being in her shoes. I am sure between the fear and the pain, things are about to hit the fan.

III

February 15 (Continued)

Baby, this is going to be short. I don't know what I can do, I can't move and the pains are overwhelming. Luckily, there seems to be some time before you pop out, so there is hope. The contractions seem to be random, I have been keeping track, it seems about 20 or 25 minutes apart.

I still don't know what that sound is in the back of the store. Although, I thought I heard something move closer. I don't smell anything or hear any of the groans that seem to follow those creatures, so I doubt it is any of them. It is probably a vagrant, or hobo, or someone like us, hiding from the destruction that surrounds us out in the streets. We are somewhat safe in here, and I want to stay that way.

Hold on Eli, I am sure we will find help soon. I love you!

IV

That was short and to the point, and at least she is maintaining her spirit in the face of such desperate times. I hope Morgan gains some strength and steps up to help her. I would hate to see her have to go through childbirth alone. That would definitely suck and likely be even more painful.

Speaking of pain, I need to take my medication and charge my computer. I am at 16 percent, and I don't have a chord near me. I would hate to get started on another account and lose power. That would definitely transport me to a place that would bring the voices back. Right now, I think I drove them away with the playlist of mellow and alternative classics.

Good night everyone, I will try to return tomorrow and maybe knock out a few more of the accounts. I don't have many left, so the end is definitely near.

CHAPTER THIRTY-TWO

"AND GOD SHALL WIPE AWAY ALL TEARS FROM THEIR EYES..."

NOVEMBER 24

I wish I could have held out longer last night and continued with the project. Unfortunately, through the emotions contained in the events, those cries and tears that plague me started to return and I had to snuff them out before they drove me closer to that padded cell in Summit View. I do find it a bit ironic that the only mental institution that remains in the state sits in Summit View. I can't help but feel that something is pulling me toward that oppressed community and I'm not sure what it is.

I'm really not sure about anything that is happening around me anymore. I feel like I am lost is some type of dimensional shift where nothing makes sense. I know some call it the Mandela Effect, where parts of the population share false memories. I'm not sure about what is real and not real. That's right you damn bastards, its Berenstein Bears not Berenstain Bears, I know it is. Please stop fucking with our sanity and us. Don't know what I am talking about, look up the Mandela Effect, and there are so many subtle changes that it is hard to keep track of them all.

I wish that this outbreak were just a false-shared memory. That is what those devious physicians at the clinic try to tell us. They keep pushing the narrative that none of this happened; that those of us affected by these memories suffered through an accidental discharge of a mind-altering toxin from one of the last steel plants in the region. Yeah right, that just fits with the globalist agenda of sending more of our jobs to China or India for cheap labor under the guise of environmental protection. If the majority of people in the United States were awake, they would see that this is just another power play from the elite.

Hell, if you dig into the detail of climate change, you will find that scientist at The National Oceanic and Atmospheric Administration (NOAA) were caught falsifying climate change data to meet directives established by the Scotereo Administration to back new tax regulations. That's right, they manipulated the data to take more money from your pockets, and rape the country of even more jobs and potential growth opportunities.

Well enough of my rambling today, I must get back to these accounts. I have to continue with explaining what happened, so the signs will be known in the future. I hope it is never needed, but I am sure Orwell thought the same thing when *1984* was released. He really could have never foreseen the contempt that the governments would show for their populations and the way society would be manipulated. In many ways, we are living inside a dystopian world and

1984 is one of the blueprints (along with *Rules for Radicals,* but that is a conversation for a different day). There is an answer for the elites and their disdain for society, and that is 1776.

Speaking of a battle, I wonder what Morgan has decided to do. I would hate to be in her shoes, the decisions she must make could weigh on her soul forever. I can honestly say, I don't know what I would do in this situation. And, I'm not sure that there is a right answer to make.

I

Hello up there, are you okay? What's wrong, can I help you? I called to her, no answer. Maybe she is one of those creatures; maybe she is trying to draw me in before gorging herself on my flesh. Fuck that, I need some air. Fuck, why do I keep talking to myself? Am I going fucking insane, why didn't she answer? I am alive and not looking down at these events from an astral plain, right? I need some air; maybe the cart return area will let me peer outside, I'm not even sure if the have doors. I can't believe she didn't hear me. I will have to try again. Yep, once I look outside, I will come back and try to reach her again.

We just may be in luck that looks like a Med Express across the street. I'm sure there are no doctors or nurses there, but the office should be better equipped to deliver a fucking baby than the Wal-Mart. Oh shit, what is that. No, not them, its those bastards from downtown. We will have to try to get out of here without being seen. That side street may work. Fuck, its one of those damn creatures. We won't be able to go that way. We definitely need to get out if here, if those soldiers

*zero in on him, we will be caught in the crossfire.
Plus, with the affinity for fire, shit!*

*Hello, I hope you can hear me, but we have to
move and fast! I can see that you aren't quite up
to speed, but we are going to have some unwanted
company. Shit, your're in labor. Fuck, I was hoping
that I was imagining that. There is a Med Express
across the street. Hopefully, we can slide out of
here while that battalion comes after the flesh-eater
coming through the parking lot.*

*I'm Morgan by the way, nice to meet you. Don't
be offended by this, but you picked one Hell of a
time to go into fucking labor. Couldn't you have
just barricaded yourself somewhere. Sorry, just
a bit overwhelmed by the situation and panic is
starting to set in. I don't know if you believe in God
or religious, but if not, this would be a great time
to put that journal down and start praying. What
the fuck am I doing? We need to get out of here and
fast. Trust me, those soldiers will shoot first and
never ask questions. If you want to live, and have
that baby, follow me.*

II

I can't believe what is happening, talk about some
bad luck. Incredibly, that strange military squadron
is there. I still have no clue where they came from
or their allegiance. Morgan definitely recognized
them, which means they are the ones responsible
for murdering the civilians trapped in the building.
They definitely need to get out of there.

I hate to tell you what I just discovered. Trust me,
it pains me as well. I just realized that the following
few lines are the last ones in Gabrielle's journal.
While I'm not reading anything into that fact, I do

find it troubling. I just hope that Gabrielle, Morgan, and especially Eli survived this encounter. One of the things I am going to search for (besides more information on the *Revelation of Moloch*) will be the birth records from this period to see if I can find either Gabrielle or Eli.

February 15 (Continued)

Eli, there may be a God after all. There is a woman in here with us and is going to help us escape and make it to the medical facility across the street. The next time I write in this journal, you will be in my arms. Remember that I love you and always will.

III

I don't know what to think. I have never been a parent, so maybe she is just overwhelmed raising Eli on her own. I have heard that kids take up all of your extra time. Maybe she just stopped journaling and recording her thoughts. It would be much easier just to talk with him. Who knows, she may have found Isaac as well, and they could be living happily somewhere in the city.

While I debated stopping there for the night, I decided that I wanted to dive one more time into our lone zombie and see what he is up to. I have to wonder if he is the one that Morgan saw approaching the Wal-Mart. Yes, that would be a coincidence, but there is certainly some type of connection between him and Gabrielle. One can only wonder if that type of connection exists. Maybe if you love someone enough, you can feel their pain, and experience the swirling mess of emotions. I have never really experienced that, but it could happen.

(Click) *Gabrielle, are you near? Is it you that haunts me in these times of solitude? I can hear a vague whisper of a dream I can almost remember and inside that dream is the lingering warmth of a forgotten touch. I know you are here somewhere. I can feel you in the darkness. While I am not the man you may remember on the outside, on the inside, I still find solace in the quiet moments of times I can barely recall.*

As much as I would love change everything that has taken place between us, I understand that this new reality will cause you to push the limits of reason. But, I can still feel your love. It calls to me, urging me to cry out in anguish and give you a sign that I am near. Unfortunately, I know my weeping cries would only echo into the nothingness that has become my world.

I should have never left, or turned my back on the providence you offered me. Our memoir was written in blood to stand the test of time much like a history that was written in stone ages ago. Unlike those authors and every figure of antiquity that has faded away to the unknown, I don't want to face this deafening vacuum alone. I don't want to be left here to live in the shadow of a wraith and I don't want to fear the visions of what once was or a lost wish of what could have been.

I know it, and understand what I have lost, as I pray it remains still, waiting for me to discover it once more in the blackness of my empty soul. Gabrielle, will you really leave here alone to unearth the secrets held inside this tainted vault that was once my heart? I cannot stand the thought of not having you in my life, if that were to come to pass, I would be left as an undefined impression of all the possibilities that I previously held dear. I will become the void that ironically, I have always been a part of and have tried desperately to escape.

Our eternal love is a promise that has existed since the dawn of thought and a gift inherent in the very fabric of our souls. Today, that bond is shrouded by the actions of the depraved and the lies of those sworn to protect our affection. Deep inside, I know I am dead, and the memories of our once powerful love are concealed in ghostly images of all that should have been. I am trapped within the silence I hear it through the veil of time where your words reverberate in my core and I quiver, though in fear or anticipation, I cannot be sure.

Gabrielle, where are you? I want to reach out and grab you. I want you to understand how I feel inside. But, instead, I know there is an unseen specter lurking over my shoulder. This phantom has siphoned hope and left me with a dream I can almost touch. With every step, it visits the edge of my memories and lines them with silver and taunts me while my mind tries to take me back to you and our past. And its vanishing countenance stays with me through every breath.

If you are here darling, please give me a sign. For I don't want to live any longer if, I cannot have you in my arms again. You are and always will be everything, and I will never stop searching for you. I love you. **(Click)**

IV

No more, please stop, I can't take anymore of this tonight. I once felt that way, but that vile beast took her from me. The way it crawled over her, the way it dug his nails into her flesh, fuck! God, now it's those fucking voices. Why did they come back? Fuck, kill me already, I am nothing, and I have nothing. Fuck!

**CHAPTER
THIRTY-THREE**

"FOR THE LORD GOD GIVETH THEM LIGHT: AND THEY SHALL REIGN FOR EVER AND EVER..."

NOVEMBER 25

I am so sorry about last night, I did not expect those accounts to hit me so hard. I am really worried about Gabrielle; I don't want to think about what could have happened to her. It honestly pains me just sitting here with no idea of her whereabouts or her fate that awaited her after leaving the store. I hope that she is safe. No, I pray she is.

As I look the notes and tapes sitting before me, I am pretty sure that this will be one of our last nights together and I cannot help but feel a shroud of sadness overwhelm me. True, I have no idea whether this manuscript will be published or if anyone will actually read this, but I have developed a sort of kinship with all of you, my potential readers.

I often sit in the dark when the visions and voices leave me alone and wonder what question you would have if we were ever to meet. I am sure I missed something, and you would call me on it. It has been extremely hard keeping track of everything considering the war that is raging inside my mind on a daily basis. I have no clue sometimes what made in onto these pages. It could be a mass conglomeration of confusion.

I have looked back at the manuscript a few times, but in each case, the nightmares start to come back and I don't want to relive any of those moments. The images are so vivid and many of the accounts inside this document hit too close to home. Sometimes, there are moments where I wish I were dead, instead of suffering through the misery I have been trapped inside. Hell, maybe Gabrielle and Eli are both better off dead instead of surviving in this shithole of a nation that we have become under the spineless leadership of a traitor. I for one wish I never witnessed half of what I did after the outbreak, I would be much more upbeat about where we are as a society.

Who knows, things could be moving in the right direction. At least now, America started to wake up and is standing against the establishment on both sides of the aisles. It may be too late, we could have used this engagement a few decades ago. I know I for one would have gladly sacrificed everything to stop the globalist infringement on our way of life.

Looking at what I have left, I think that I will start of the night with our religious man and his disciples. I wonder; did he find the martyr? Was he able to find the chosen one and baptize him upon the altar? Having travelled to many of the locations that I have written about, I can't figure out where all of this was supposed to take place. I can't find any statue or structure that could be used as a shrine or altar. Pittsburgh definitely isn't Rome or one of the ancient metropolitan areas full of artwork or great artists. Yes, we had Drella, but his greatness is argued more than accepted.

I

And the Lord spoke to the prophet,
Behold, the Martyr, the Fornicator,
and the Sinner stand before the pyre,
Look into their souls, for inside their
true self will be revealed,
And the guardian will bow before thee,
begging for deliverance.

(The Revelation of Moloch 13.6)

Followers, look upon that passage, as Thy Father foretold, a man approaches from the East. His festering rot is visible, and his body will serve for a proper sacrifice. Reach out for him, impale him, and allow him to embrace his destiny upon the sacred staff. Through his tears of blood and delicious entrails, we will feast for all eternity next to the father.

Remain steadfast in your faith, for the scent of another is close and the whore walks beside her. Look around you, search through the frozen embers of snow, and find the fornicator and the sinner. For their bodies must be cleansed of their impurities, and their bile discarded unto the fiery well beneath this new Babylon.

Thy Father has spoken truths throughout our journey, and through his divinity, our oasis will appear once the Messiah has been baptized in the blood of the unholy trinity that stand before us. Raise the mighty scepters to the Lord our Father and batter them until the lowest depths of sanctuary echo with the sounds of their pleas.

Ready the fires and reveal the blessed altar above the pit, for the prophesized one is upon us.
Let us pray.

Lord of Light
Our passage to Mecca is complete
and your masterpiece waits
Open your heart to our final sacrifice
And give is the eternal blessing
For we stand here in awe of your power
And inspired by your wisdom
When we started this journey, we were not worthy
But through your power, we have been healed
In Your Name, We Pray
Amen

II

Oh God, was our religious leader part of that squadron? Was he the leader? No, it can't be. There is something saintly with him and his followers; there has been nothing military about him throughout these pages. This can't be. Something else must be taking place. This can't be at the Wal-Mart. No, fuck, this can't be real. Fuck, that is the last page of material from the journalist. There has to be more somewhere. No, this can't be happening.

Damn, all I have left is one recording from our lover boy. Maybe he will be somewhere else and not part of this encounter in the parking lot. Dammit, I hope that is the case; I couldn't imagine everything ending this way. If it did, I might just have to sacrifice myself. I don't know how I could wake tomorrow and face the world. I would be miserable.

(Click) Finally, the beauty blesses me from my visions. Gabrielle, finally our passions can be one.

As I look upon you, I see your pain and feel your breath. But why, are you standing before those men. Are they hurting you? I can hear your weep among the screams and your faint voice stirs, so soft, so pure, inside my mind.

Do not fear; I am here for you. I will protect you from the demonic horde that stands peering into your depths. I can see our salvation in the distance, as a brilliant light illuminates the darkness. You can feel it too, in the newfound hope that flows through your veins, as your screams grow shallow. All of the images and truths are one and countless feelings grow to what could be inside each other's arms.

Gabrielle, I long for your touch, but cannot comprehend the visions that stand before me. What my dear, is happening to you? I cannot bear to see the pain in your eyes. Where did that dagger come from? The splattered blade rising from the dominion held deep within your soul. As the tiny hand reaches for the heavens, I can see it pierce your abdomen from the inside. The razors protruding from his mouth, our son is alive.

Look at the way he holds you, feasting on the intestinal ropes that nourished him through this ordeal. Look at the way he swims inside your exposed womb, his eyes sparkling among the flames. He stands next to you, drinking from the sanguine river flowing down your breasts. Gabrielle, he is beautiful, glowing like a sacred angel on high. Gabrielle, he is perfect, and now shares a most distinguished bond with both of us.

Gabrielle, I am sorry I could not protect you. But, I swear before the Lord, I will protect our son. In the distance, a lone scream is heard, as the silence in my mind grows louder. The candles upon the tainted altar flicker, shadows fade, and I know that for once, this sacrifice was just.

III

Nooooo! This can't be! Nooooo! This cannot be happening! Noooo!

EPILOGUE

"HE WHICH TESTIFIETH THESE THINGS SAITH..."

Two weeks have passed since I last sat at my computer and worked on anything. In many ways, I can't believe that our journey has ended and I will not be sitting down with you every night. Plus, I am still in shock over what transpired. I have so many questions, but many of those will be left unanswered. Don't worry, I will not forget about you. No matter what happens over time, I will continue the search for more material to add to the blog, so you can have more accounts for you to digest. What I ventured into is something that I can't stop working on, this information is too important just to let it go.

I already started as I reached out to an antique book dealer, Richard Blake; from a small town the outer reaches of New England who specializes in the rare occult and religious books from all eras of antiquity. I had hoped that he could point me in the direction of a complete copy of *the Revelation of Moloch*. While he has heard of this manuscript and had a couple of random passages, he didn't have a full document on hand.

He did, however, know of a book that may include this Gospel. According to Blake, the *Daemonum Codex Illustrationis*, a mysterious religious text translated as the *Demonic Codex of Enlightenment* that was discovered near the remnants of Levant, may have contained this legendary piece of scripture. The last know whereabouts of the book was inside the Cathedral of Neceadonia, the religious epicenter for a strange nomadic cult based in southwestern Pennsylvania. Unfortunately, no one has heard of them since early in the 1900s, and the organization seemed to vanish.

With this project complete and having nothing better to do right now, I think I am going to dive into this group and the legendary Man of Cloth from over in Summit View over the next few weeks. I hope that I can find some information on them. I love researching mysteries and finally have the energy to take on another project.

I also wanted to pass on that there has still been no contact from Natalie and all of us at the clinic have begun to fear the worse. None of us can imagine what happened to her; it seems like she has disappeared into thin air. Personally, there is part of me, something deep inside, that wants her to return and join me for our next date. Now that I am done writing this, finding a companion to share my life would be awesome and could help me maintain my sanity.

It also appears that the visions and voices that tormented me throughout this project have gone; so, this may be the perfect time try to enter into a relationship. Everything is going smoothly, in fact, I have cut back on my medication and seem to be functioning better than I can remember. Honestly, I feel better now than I have in years. It is as if a giant weight has been removed from my shoulders and has allowed my sanity to return.

Maybe all of the doctors and therapists were right, and it was the accounts that drove me into that downward spiral into darkness and misery. If that's the case, I am happy to be done with it. Although, I know that I will never forget about what took place during the outbreak. How could I, this plague destroyed my life and stole my soul mate? I know that she didn't deserve to die and we, as a society, didn't deserve the torture.

I only hope that once this manuscript is out there, more people can come to terms with what they witnessed and hopefully some of the sheep wake to the globalist agenda that continues to torment us. Every day, more of the plan is being exposed and more of the corruption being brought to light. Unfortunately, it is us, the population, which must continue to stand and fight. With the mainstream media of our nation betraying our founding principles, we the people have a responsibility to stand against their lies.

I would like to think that in some way, this project has helped the cause and will give people the courage to stand up and create a testament for the blind to see once again. While I'm sure many will ignore it, the dark truths held within these pages should be used to enlighten the masses to the dangers behind seemingly innocent words such as sustainability and progress or popularized plans such as Agenda 21 or Agenda 2030. I know that these words may sound harmless, but they are all about control.

Of course, you must first be willing to accept that you are the enemy of the elite before any of this makes sense to you. I came to grips with that long ago. There was one day after the Gulf War during a NATO exercise in Albania. The media manipulation our government used to protect this country for political and financial gain would make anyone question the true allegiances in play. All I will say is that they differed from what many would expect.

Today, I am content with. Fuck, who's at my door now? Hold on for a second, probably that pizza guy again. If it is, I am going to lose my mind, how hard is it to get a fucking address right. What the fuck, what would they say that for? Trust me; there is no one here except me. Fuck you, man. There is no one screaming in here. Hell, it's been quite a while since I heard anything but the sound of my voice.

That's so fucked, they wanted me to shut the kid up, and they even threatened to call the police. Fucking bastards ruined my train of thought. Damn them. Oh God, no, not a headache. I thought they were gone. See what they did, that asshole at the door, they fucking woke the beasts. The screams, the cries, no go away. Please go away. I did what you wanted; I finished your story. Please, Renae, take them away. You killed Morgan; you took Natalie, Just make them stop. I'm sorry that I couldn't save you. I know, I deserved to die, not you, and I can't change what happened. Please, baby, you must stop haunting me, one of us had to live, one of us needed to watch over Eli.

I'm sorry, just please stop! Shut up Eli; I don't have any more food, wasn't she enough. Please stop crying, I can't take it anymore, and I can't afford to move again. Please stop, I beg you, please. Pleeeeaaaassseeee!

APPENDIX

THE REVELATION OF MOLOCH

One of the most interesting parts of this manuscript has been my work translating the pieces of scripture from Latin to English. Unfortunately, I haven't been able to find Revelation of Moloch in its entirety anywhere. All I have is the pieces I documented inside the book and a few other passages that I have pieced together from the some research and conversations with people outside of the area. I wish I could have the entire Gospel, I would love to read it; and I will continue to search for it until I die. Until I find more passages and upload them to the blog, here is the original Latin scripture from the accounts of our Man of Cloth before my translations, as well as some of the other passages that were not part of my source material.

Revelation Molech,

Et commota est terra et erit dies in qua prophetia vivetis. Damnatorum et sola formidatis ibi conprehendet audiatur clamor ortus ut satelles. (1.11)

In die ortus trans flumen purus. Diculam basi nostri salvatores in montem offendunt. Lacrimas fundit munus sola in paradiso. Vox cantantis in gemitu et peccatores novae urbi attulere. (2.13)

Itaque hoc die, a series sub Maximo Confluentes curru ferri. Vi erumpentium Vesuvii et angelos flebis. Cinere triangulum aureum Christus apparebit. Ad hoc ut terram tuam Sanctum sanctorum. Et tu exsultabis in fonte in remissionem peccatorum. (2.10)

Potens est et contremuit terra. Ejicient te ab infidelibus in illum hiatum aeneumque flammae haberet. Peccatorum mundati ad dexteram Patris. Magna os suum bestiae ad radices montis. Et risit ad desperationem. (3.13)

Filius Dei audisti profitendi sapientiam massa. Ecce quantum iter damnatione dignus. Hecate per os tuum ad solemnitatem satelles specu. Ibi filicemque stipatus robore magno ianuam aperuit. Et una electa ad introitum vestrum manet. (7.28)

Et propheta ad Patrem. Ultra in bivio vitae est derecta potestatem a venalicium de antiquitate. Transite per generationes perditis haberi, ut in praesepio. Praedictum adventum tuum. (7.9)

Ex intimis procedunt fulgura, Geysers sanguinis clamat infinita Memphis angustiae cotidianae Exsulis immortui bestiae surrexerunt et ambulaverunt ante thronum. Surgunt animae septem septem man- mala pestis per caput et sanguinem perditum splendebit lumen et lux erit ut redemptionis. (8.12)

Custodiebant autem filius potentium sol montis desit vox visio reponi intrinsecus murmura caelum erat enim prope frater, salutem et propior. (9.10)

Imo tenebris et sole ad Omnipotentem flevit. Et posuit animam meam in vitam tuam per novum modum propter signa vitae surgunt et fortius crescit prophetavit. (9.12)

Samael dehiscunt, et Prometheus, ut ridet, remissionem in aeternum, spiritum accedentem. Per sanguinem et spurcum euripus est urbs sola salus moto et animas clamant legionis. (10.1)

Sicut in Apostolis orandum indicem Domini martyris sola diversa tradit clamore valido merula propter sanguinem Agni, et adest uiam salutis ultima resurrexit in austro. (10.10)

Per clamoribus aegrum prophetis somno Caelo et Inferno, et commovebuntur simulacra prae timore clamaverunt paenitentiam agite adpropinquavit enim Filius hominis carina Angustiae maestitiam compositus et foeda plaudit damnatione peccantium fleret Patrem omnipotentem. (10.13)

Sicut scriptum est in profundis tenebris primogenitus baptizo in vini fortis ascensionis: Accipite, et bibite, hic est sanguis meus, per sacrificium Christi iuvenes ordinetur. (11.2)

Locutusque est Dominus ad prophetam: Ecce martyris fornicator et peccator sto ante rogum:

Respice in animarum suarum, pro semetipso
intra revelabitur, et adorabunt in conspectu tuo
tutori, petens liberari. (13.6)

Other Passages from
The Revelation of Moloch

These are what I believe are the first two lines of
the Gospel. I actually found these two passages at
an antique store on a strange picture/postcard that
appears to be from the effigy used in the Cremation
of Care Ritual. The first passage will be in its original
Latin form, with the translation directly below it.

Apocalypsis Luciferus perditionis, quae per
haec dicit Dominus exercituum tenebris
operta discipulis suis tradere sacra symbola
temptationibus quae inluminat laci quasi
cadaver putridum et vox resonat in Angustiae,
ac beata Seraphim Molech squalore torpebant.
(1.1) Quis dicere uerba referre viros et
inambulabo inter Patrem et Filium Deum et
testimonium Luciferus perditionem: quoniam
omnia quae sunt. (1.2)

The Revelation of Luciferus Perdition, which
The Lord Almighty passed through the
darkness, to deliver his veiled disciples symbols
of the sacred trials, which shall illuminate the
pit; and his voice echoed in the canyon, and the
blessed seraph Moloch awoke. (1.1) Who dare
walk among men and recount the messages of
the Father, and the testimony of his divine son
Luciferus Perdition, for all things that must be.
(1.2)

Mr. Blake from the antique bookstore was able to provide me with two more passages.

Et ecce oblitus sub signo signavi et vitio sceptrum ululatus Obruit auster testis flebile et luna in sanguinem. (6.12) Et infernus cataracta a fletu, et coram Patre risit blasphemus scitis nomen eius victimis et praedici posse. (6.13)

And behold, under the sign of the forgotten seal, and, the tainted scepter, a howling wind overwhelmed the witness, and the moon wept tears of blood. (6.12) And those tears fell like a waterfall into the inferno, and the Father smiled at the sight of the blasphemer, for his name was known and his sacrifice foretold. (6.13)

Made in the USA
Columbia, SC
27 September 2017